ReD SToCKiNG SOCIETY

Secret of the S-Game

a novel by
ACE PASSMORE

CHANGING LIVES PRESS

Published by:
Changing Lives Press
www.changinglivespress.com

Library of Congress Cataloging in Publication data
is on file with the publisher.

ISBN-13: 978-1-73225-840-2

I greatly appreciate the editorial assistance of Angelle Pilkington, Toby Osborne, Bill Bailey, and Donna Passmore who never ceases to amaze me.

Cover Art by Tobin Pilotte

Printed & bound in the United States of America.

10   9   8   7   6   5   4   3   2   1

To Donna, Starr, Jackie, Skye, Grant, Diane, Mom & Dad, Grimp, Ellory, Junie, Ines, Ondine, and grandkids to come. Thanks for listening to the story about *S2* and *Red Stockings* every Christmas until we got it right. Your belief in me has helped create wonder and magic.

AUTHOR'S FOREWORD

I know from experience that kids 8–10 years old begin doubting the existence of Santa Claus. When I was that age, I calculated that he would have to visit millions of households per hour worldwide to deliver his bag of treasure, which is highly unlikely. My parents assured me that Santa magic trumps logic, appeasing my curiosity until I learned a great secret. You see, Santa resides in both fantasy and reality—alive for kid believers but also for grown-ups with golden hearts. Yes, **S1**—real Santa—exists, and the old boy still works odd hours. I know this since I'm an S2. Puzzled? For the first time ever, inspired by real events from my past, the Santa game is explained in one adventurous story that will gratify kids 9–90. With millions of players globally, each an important cog, it's all about giving and creating wonder. If you open your heart and mind to it, Santa Magic will reach out and tap you on the shoulder when you least expect it. Long live the S-Game!

—Ace Passmore, S2

"As empires rise and fall,
St. Nick survives them all."
—MR. ROY MABREY, S2 ROYALE

"Good sparks good . . ."
—WAHOO JAMES, S2

ReD
SToCKiNG
SOCIETY

PROLOGUE

"**H**unk of junk!" I snapped while brushing snow from the seat of my clunker bike and shaking frozen gunk from the frame. But what could I expect from an old rust bucket anyway?

"See ya, Bub, stay outta trouble!" my zany friend Sean called out as he climbed into his mom's flashy SUV. I usually waited until everyone had exited the carpool line to claim my lame two-wheel ride, but it was too cold today. Nodding good-bye to Sean, I yelled, "Only if you do!" As the vehicle pulled away, I couldn't help noticing the stack of presents visible through the back window. Only two weeks until Christmas—Sean was hitting the jackpot again, lucky guy.

I pushed my squeaky wheels past the line of cars and out of sight to the rear parking lot, laughing to myself on the way. Maybe Santa would bring me a brand-new bike for Christmas. Then Tooth Fairy would deliver a cell phone for my twelfth birthday on New Year's Eve. And to top it off, Easter Bunny would materialize a new flat-screen TV in my basket. *Yeah, right.*

I'd just started pedaling when I heard my kid brother Chad holler, "Hey, wait up, Bub!" Chad's green eyes sparkled under his beanie as he trudged through the fresh snow.

As I waited, a pimpled punk named Jake flipped snow in my face and smirked . . . bummer. Back then it was the story of my life. If only I'd been a superhero, but no such luck.

"What's up, bro?" I asked Chad, just a fourth grader who usually took the bus home.

"Missed the bus, darn it!" he said, grinning like a clown. I shook my head and smiled. Chad had been nagging Mom forever to let him walk home with me, but she figured he was too young. The kid didn't even have a clunker bike to call his own.

"Dare to ride the handlebars?" I asked.

"Nah. Those rusty bars won't hold a mouse," Chad shot back.

"What? You doubt my metal marvel?" I playfully kicked his boot, then began pedaling to match his slow pace.

The snow under my tires crunched like dry cereal as we started for home. Old Man Winter was in a grumpy mood that year and had punished our town with heavy snow. Despite dressing warmly, my fingers and toes were frozen pipes. The streets were practically empty, most everyone indoors and warm by the fire. Not even four o'clock, but already the sun was sliding behind a patch of brooding storm clouds on the horizon.

We made our way down Main Street, past Yellow Flower Loop, and up Carson Street toward the train tracks, my bike squeaking and creaking every inch of the way. The only thing louder than the groaning frame was the raucous barking of Bugsy, the mongrel who guarded Rex's Auto Salvage. He wasn't that big, but his feistiness made up for size.

Chad slowed to a crawl as we neared the growling dog.

"Worried about that old mutt?" I asked, trying to stay cool. Usually I rode past here faster than greased lightning. Bugsy was renowned for his filthy fur, halo of flies, and dose of attitude.

"Can't we go another way?" Chad pleaded, now trembling as he adjusted his backpack.

"Might be too late for that," I answered. We could see Bugsy trailing along his side of the fence, barking fiercely and jumping up on hind legs. His sharp teeth dripping with saliva, he curled his lip with a menacing growl, then backed up ready to clear the fence in one leap.

I could hear my heart beating in my ears . . . decision time. "Make a run for it, Chad," I ordered. "I'll distract Bugsy!" Chad was halfway down the block before I could finish my sentence. *Thanks a lot, brother.* As if ready to attack, Bugsy let out a warning yelp, then leaped the fence like an Olympian—a stinky, dirty one.

"Come and get me, fur face!" I yelled. Pedaling hard, I made a sharp left, spraying Bugsy with dirty slush. Wrong move.

The beast rose to the challenge—our road race was on! Pounding paws slipped and slid behind me. Would I make it home or end up chilled roadkill?

"Faster!" I urged. Pedal, pedal, pedal . . . bike, don't fail me now. Then, as if on cue, I heard a ping—a spoke popped out on my back tire—followed by a terrible rattle. Really? My bike was ready to quit so soon? I wanted to toss it over the fence and let it rust in the salvage yard. But Bugsy was almost nipping at my heels, his sewer breath enough to gag a maggot.

I thought about circling around to give Chad a bigger lead, but with a rattling bike, I had to change course to slow Bugsy down. Luckily, the road ran alongside woods with a twisty stream cutting through it. All of the older kids biked below in the summer and launched over the water using an ancient wooden ramp. If I could make it across, I'd leave Bugsy panting on this side with my house only a shortcut away on the other side.

Yes!

Without a second thought, I swerved off-road and down a slippery hill toward the tree line. It was slicker than expected, and snow was getting stuck between my remaining spokes. I heard another ping as a second spoke bit the dust. What else could go wrong?

I pedaled faster and stole a look over my shoulder. Bugsy with his short legs was struggling with deep snow, until we were beneath tree branches sheltering us like white umbrellas. Less than a bicycle-length apart now, I was sucking air and blowing fog while Bugsy wheezed like a bad accordion. Suddenly, there it was—the river.

And the ramp too, looking ricketier than ever, but no turning back now. As the barking machine edged closer, I plowed forward with my bike screeching in protest. I felt my first tire go up the incline, then the back tire, and I was airborne . . . cold as a witch's nose.

The blanket of snow on the opposite riverbank cushioned my landing, the impact costing more spokes. As the chassis emitted another groan, I glanced back to see Bugsy skidding to a halt, staring in disbelief. He'd never seen a flying bike before. "Later, dirtball!" I shouted.

Jubilant, I chuckled as the snorting dog trotted up the riverbank. What a sore loser.

Pulling my hat down lower over my crew cut and iceberg ears, I turned toward home. Just as I began to pedal again, a distant snarl riveted me. Upstream, my new worst enemy was speeding across a fallen tree that spanned the water—a makeshift bridge. What?!

Was Bugsy a junkyard dog or a mastermind mutt? And he was grinning, not a good sign.

We were off again! I put the pedal to the metal, but within a minute he had nearly caught up, his four paws working better on uneven ground than my two half-flat tires. One vicious nip grazed my jean pocket and spurred me on. As I reached the edge of the woods, an imposing tree came into view. My oak tree. My front yard.

Home.

With a last desperate push, I propelled my old bike into the yard, jumped off, crunched over the icy grass, and scrambled up the homemade ladder nailed to the big oak. At the top, I eased onto my favorite branch and panted, trying to catch my breath in the frigid air.

Peering down, I started taunting Bugsy who was leaping and barking in rage.

"Bub! You made it!" Chad yelled from the front porch, then scooted into the house.

Instantly, my dad, Ron, shot out of the side door and limped fast, waving his crutches at my attacker. "Shoo! Out of here!" One crutch gently prodded Bugsy who got the message.

As he padded away, Bugsy sniffed over my bike—recognizing junk—and delivered the final insult. Lifting his leg, he piddled right on the handlebars.

Despicable dog! I burned for revenge.

"Come on down, Bub—safe now," Dad urged.

"Thanks, Dad!" I exclaimed, watching Bugsy disappear from sight.

"No problem." He squinted and pointed to my upper lip. "Growing more peach fuzz, son?"

"Dad, please!" I said, horrified. "You've reminded me ten million times. At least."

"That's a lot. Okay, Bub, sorry. Anyway, Chad said Bugsy's big as a wolf. He's just a runt."

"Well, maybe he exaggerated some . . . family trait, as you say."

Dad grinned as I descended fast and, sidestepping yellow snow, kicked my clunker on the way over to him. "Sir, my bike's busted bad. Can I please get a new one for Christmas? I really need it—not an exaggeration."

Dad clenched his jaw. "Bub, uh . . . actually . . . we need to discuss that over the weekend. Christmas might be a little different this year."

That's when Chad reappeared on the front porch and started heaving snowballs! Dad and I retaliated before he waved us inside where Mom cheerily greeted us.

It turned out that my father was correct—this Christmas would be different. But as I entered our warm, modest home, I had no inkling that one of us would soon face a danger far beyond Bugsy . . . not to mention unravel a great mystery, confront a ghost, and help create magic.

Me.

But I'm jumping way ahead of myself. . . .

CHAPTER 1

In case anyone doubted Christmas was around the corner, that Sunday Mom put out seasonal plates decorated with cartoony reindeer pulling Santa around on his sleigh. In my opinion, it was fantasy overload.

"Hello, aren't we a bit old for those, Mom?" I said while cracking my knuckles. I was almost twelve, waaay past believing a red-suited chubby guy circles the globe without GPS or oxygen, delivering tons of toys in a single day. Why did parents keep up the charade year after year?

As Mom set down the last plate in front of herself, she replied: "Well, don't inspect it, just eat from it. We don't live in a museum, you know." She was more frazzled than usual, her frizzy hair standing on end like she'd received another shock from our erratic toaster.

"I like 'em," Chad said, trying to crack his knuckles too. "Feels like Santa's on his way."

Mom smiled and pecked Chad's forehead. "Wash your hands, boys, and no more knuckles."

St. Nick and his antlered friends were soon smothered by a plop of meatloaf with a side of veggies. As usual, Dad led the conversation. "So, Chad, how was your class holiday party?" Chad launched into a looong story as my mind wandered while pushing carrots around.

In the distance, Dad's words barely registered. "Eat your carrots, guys, good for vision. You never see a rabbit wearing glasses." I ignored his drab stab at humor, lost inside my own world.

Me with Sean and the gang at the ramp by the river. Awesome summer day, me on my gleaming custom red Schwinn bike, jumping off the ramp and doing a perfect 360 over the river. All the girls swooning—

"Young man, are you daydreaming again?"

I snapped to attention. "Sorry, Dad. What's up?"

Dad leaned back in his chair, drawing in a deep breath. With hands behind his balding head, he shifted his broken leg until the plaster cast peeked out from under the table. "It's important to know we're having a lean Christmas this year."

I glanced over at Chad. When had he finished the story about his class party? My little brother's usually bright face—resting beneath a mop of scruffy, sandy hair—dimmed like a broken light bulb. "How lean?" I asked, imagining a slightly less shiny Schwinn.

"Scanty, I suppose, is the right word."

"What does 'scanty' mean?" Chad asked.

"It, um, means we need to tighten our belts," Dad said with a wince as he bent over and tried to scratch his leg through the cast. "Since I lost my job at the plant—you know, after the auto accident—we haven't saved much money. We're down but not out."

"So, no new bike for me?" I asked, trying not to frown.

Mom sighed as she messed with her hair, surprisingly finding a pencil amid the tangled curls. "You know I've been working two jobs to make ends meet until Dad heals up. I just wish it were enough . . . for a special Christmas." Her eyes moistened while Dad stared hard at the salt shaker on the table. We all hated to see Mom sad.

"But," Chad piped in, trying to stay upbeat, "there'll still be Santa gifts, right?"

Mom barely nodded and rubbed her nose. Dad kept staring down the shaker. Chad turned to me to fill the void, but I was finding salt fascinating too.

Dad came to life. "We still have a little money stashed away." He meant in the tin box inside a kitchen drawer, labeled: Property Ron & Chris Olney. They called it the Kitchen Kitty, but it was really just whatever remained after bills and groceries were paid. Dad cleared his throat. "Although, with me laid up now and who knows what medical costs might arise, we really need to—"

"Be scanty?" I interrupted, aware of my last "Kitty peek" showing a mere $400.

Dad nodded sheepishly, staring at his leg like it was a curse.

"Guess I'll be waiting another century for a new bike," I grumbled, rising from the dinner table. "May I be excused?"

"Me too," said Chad.

Mom nodded. "Clear your plates."

My parents sat at the table, exchanging awkward looks, their nightly ritual for months. I had to escape the dungeon, go stretch my legs. Chad needed it too . . . poor guy. He was only ten—and just barely.

"Can we walk down to Grant's?" Maybe drooling over the stock in the bike shop's window would pep up Chad. Besides, easy access to Main Street was the only perk of living in this old part of town instead of newer areas like most of my schoolmates.

Dad checked his watch. "Stay on familiar streets, back by dusk, no talking to strangers. Love you guys."

I nodded to Chad, who seemed happy to be taking a stroll with his big bro. After decking ourselves out in full winter garb, we charged out the holiday-adorned door into the white swirls of a snow flurry.

Mom and Dad stood in the doorway, watching us leave, holding hands . . . their usual.

Chad was short and chunky, while I was tall and wiry. After a quick dusting from the elements, we were transformed into an odd pair of snowmen who'd just sprung to life, cruising down the street. "Real bummer about Christmas, huh?" I nudged Chad.

"Yeah, but Santa will visit. Always does."

"Well, this year don't expect anything with a big bow on it." I wanted to say more but bit my tongue.

Chad pouted while gazing back at the long line of decorated, unlit street lamps. "It's not fair," he finally said.

I couldn't argue.

At that moment, we passed a fancy house with a huge Christmas tree in the window—twinkling lights, glass ornaments, silver angel on top . . . glorious. Our tree at home was a Thrift-Mart

4

model, only four feet tall, with spindly, fake branches . . . no comment.

"Sometimes, I wish we were rich," Chad lamented while shivering.

"Yeah, well, money's not everything," I lied. "Maybe if we stare through the window at Grant's long enough, he'll take pity and gift us bikes to ride into the sunset," I said with a wink, trying to cheer him up.

Just as Chad cracked a grin, I heard the strangest sound coming from a large, red building across the avenue. Two street lamps in front were broken, adding to the mystery of the clunking, grinding noise.

"What's that place?" I murmured, realizing I'd never noticed it before, though I'd walked the route many times. Most buildings in this part of town were old and quaint, but this was a gigantic warehouse with dozens of dark windows. Like the eyes of a spider, they all seemed to stare right at me! The hairs on the nape of my neck stood up.

Chad shook his head and continued strolling the last block to Main Street alone, as if nothing were amiss. But how could I not have spotted the hulking warehouse before? And that sound— much louder than the factory Dad used to work at. Concrete grating against concrete? Giant cogs turning? Then a heavy thud, followed by silence again.

"Hey, wait up, buddy!" I called to Chad, almost at the end of the block. Glancing back, I noticed a sign on the wrought-iron gate in front of the building: RSS, Inc. I shrugged at the meaning of the letters, just as mystifying as the shadowy structure itself.

Next was Clarke's Department Store, its big show windows lit with Christmas-themed displays . . . including Santa with elves, merry mannequins decorating trees, and skiers racing down an Alpine hill. How many wide-eyed window shoppers, including Olney clan, had stood here captivated in the past?

When I caught up with Chad, he was firmly planted in front of Grant's Bike Boutique. On Sundays, Main Street resembled a ghost town, no shoppers in sight. We were the only ones crazy enough to traipse around that day.

Suddenly, the sound of boots crunching through snow interrupted. I turned, but we were all alone—my imagination? Chad was standing still, fogging up Grant's window glass as he gawked at the colorful bikes inside. All were mechanical marvels—bells and mirrors attached to sturdy handlebars; rich leather seats atop shiny, triangular frames; and plump tires with unworn treads. I, however, only had eyes for one: my dream machine, on display, front and center.

"There she is . . ." I whispered in awe, my heart pounding. The Schwinn Crimson Crusher mountain bike, price tag $500— one for the ages. It was a custom model, not available online or anywhere else. Medium shade of red, sleek lines, aluminum frame, shiny as a new coin, with gleaming spokes and a 24-speed drivetrain. The polar opposite of my rusty and decrepit clunker. "She will be mine," I vowed, realizing its price likely exceeded our family savings.

Chad laughed. "In your dreams. Hey, I want that one too."

"No way!" I snapped back. "It's too big for you. The Crusher's my destiny. I'll make sweet jumps and leave Bugsy in the dust."

Chad shrugged as his eyes roamed to a bright blue bike in the corner. "Fine, keep your pink bike. I'll take that smaller blue one."

"You're blind as a bat. Mine's crimson, not pink. Besides, who cares what color it is? Just look at her . . . total perfection." My eyes glazed as I studied every inch of the frame—not a thing I would've changed except the price. But Chad was right; it was only a dream.

Keeping tabs on the sneaky sunset, again I had the feeling someone was watching. Out of the corner of my eye, had I glimpsed the ghostly reflection of a petite, spike-haired girl? I spun around to find us still alone on Main Street, except for store window mannequins and a Santa figure dangling above.

Strange.

"Let's get going, close to dusk," I said with chattering teeth, wrapping my arms around my chest, both cold and spooked.

"Can't we check the window display at Toby's Toys?" Chad asked hopefully. "Best marbles around, especially thumpers. Please!"

"Negatory. We've teased ourselves enough for one day."

"You really think we'll get zilch for Christmas this year, Bub? Mom and Dad always kid about misbehaving—lumps of coal—but now I think they're serious."

"Don't worry, shrimp. I'll donate my baseball mitt. Too small for me anyway."

Chad crumpled up his nose. "Why would I want that stinky, old thing?"

Pulling my brother into a playful headlock, I turned him around to face the way home. Scanning the route ahead, I saw a chain of lampposts lighting up—one after another—except for a dark patch in front of the RSS building.

In the movies, scary music would be playing and girls screaming.

"Do you hear that scraping sound?" I asked, straining my ears to detect those noises again.

"Maybe it's Santa's sleigh landing on a rooftop?" Chad said— still dreaming, still believing.

Exhaling frosty fog, I shook my head. "If so, he's scouting a bit early. C'mon, I can't feel my fingers anymore."

As we hustled back along the road, the warehouse delivered a parting shot: another loud thud. Obviously, something peculiar was going down.

Then I spotted a clue. Attached to the front roof was a small, circular sign rotating slowly, back and forth. The sign was emblazoned with two legs—one red and one black—crossing each other like a pair of swords on a big coat of arms.

But the feet didn't have toes; instead they were rounded like a pair of long socks. That's when it struck me: These were old-fashioned *stockings*. And as the sign spun one way, the stockings got smaller and smaller . . . before spinning opposite when they enlarged again. A perfect illusion—hypnotic—and I stared a moment before breaking away.

Arriving home minutes later, we stripped off our gear and warmed up by the fire. Dad hobbled in and asked us about the bikes, and Chad described his new favorite, the Blue Beast. I kept on nodding, but I wasn't really tuned in.

As I gazed into the flickering flames, my head kept replaying the crunching of snow and the image of a girl reflected in the shop window. And that intriguing warehouse with its frightening sound effects. The stuff of nightmares, yet I was drawn to it like steel to a magnet.

CHAPTER 2

The sound of toast popping up and rich aroma of Mom's coffeepot beat any alarm clock. After shaking off the cobwebs of sleep, I realized that school was out for the holidays, and I had no dragons to slay. Yessss!

Still, rather than listening to Chad dishing about the Christmas countdown and watching Dad limping around, trying to be useful, I decided to visit Grant's again. Not that I had another option, as my pile of rusty bolts imitating a bike had been laid to rest in the garage.

The walk would allow me to investigate the creepy warehouse, and then I'd convince Mr. Grant to let me test-drive the Crusher for the umpteenth time. The old cuss always scowled before nodding curtly and spouting, "Make it pronto, kid." I was allowed only to circle the showroom's waxed floors at turtle speed, but no matter. Just sitting on that comfy seat, fingers wrapped around those handlebars, I imagined how sweet it would be to take my Crusher out for an off-road trial.

And settle the score with a certain mongrel.

There was a mad dash of feet as Chad's bedroom door flew

open. Uh oh, timing off! Quickly, I was close behind, both of us in pj's racing down the stairs, shoulder to shoulder, and vying for pole position. Breakfast was always an adventure.

Sliding into our seats at the table, I reached for the single slice of buttered toast. The loser would have to wait until the next round or, on bad days, it was the last slice. In that case, the dreaded pot of porridge—aka sludge—would be waiting.

We managed to grab the slice at the same time in a brotherly tug-of-war. "It's mine, squirt!" I insisted.

"Not a chance," Chad shot back, "and don't call me squirt."

"Calm down, you two; there's a couple more slices in the toaster!" Dad roared, trying to bring sanity to chaos. "If the darn thing still works . . . keeps shorting out."

Too late. Chad's eyes slitted as he stole a monster bite of the toast.

Instantly, I released my hold and let the rest of the slice enter his filthy trap. "Brat, that's cheating."

"Nope, it's eating," he countered, his mouth full of chewed toast.

"Here you go, Bub," Dad said, placing a fresh slice on my plate. "No need for squabbling, boys." He hobbled back into the kitchen.

Chad and I glanced at the butter dish—only a dollop left. We grabbed our knives and began a swashbuckling duel for the prize.

Mom walked in just then, looking haggard in her ketch-up-stained waitress outfit, after working the graveyard shift at Danny's Diner. "No sword-fighting at the table!" she urged. "We're out of butter, so I'll make up some porridge."

Chad and I exchanged looks and mouthed the word *sludge*. Skunk stew might taste better.

Holding a screwdriver, Dad poked his head in from the kitchen where he was "fixing" the toaster again. "C'mon, guys, stop fighting. Mom's got a headache."

With that distraction, I swept the butter onto my blade, giving me the last laugh. "Dry toast for you, little bro," I said, smiling at Chad's defeated frown. Served him right for trying to one-up his big bad brother.

"Yowch!" As if an omen for the day, the lights dimmed eerily before Dad emerged, hair standing up, shaking his tingling right hand. "Got fritzed again."

Chad thumbed his nose at me as I pointed at the porridge. Another routine breakfast.

* * *

Not even an hour later, I stared in horror through the window of Grant's Bike Boutique, unable to compute what was happening. Why was the owner moving the Schwinn Crimson Crusher from its pride-of-place golden pedestal? Why was he taking a pair of scissors and snipping off the price tag? And why was he walking over to the cash register and talking so friendly to that girl?

That girl. She was strangely familiar, with her shock of pink, spiky hair. She turned to face the window as Mr. Grant counted the stack of cash just handed to him. The sunburned girl had impish blue eyes, a likable face behind her freckle patch, and a ruby stud in her button nose. Was she grinning at me?

Mr. Grant placed the wad of bills into the drawer of his old-fashioned register with a happy ka-ching! The girl, in her late teens, was dressed in ripped jeans and a leather jacket decorated with studs on the sleeves. She nodded thanks, took the handlebars of *my* bike and led it toward the door.

But this was unthinkable. How could she? Where was she going with it? And why didn't I hate her? She was about to steal my custom built, one-of-a-kind Crusher. "Noooo!"

But I didn't hate her. In fact, she looked refreshingly different from most of the so-called normal folks in our cookie-cutter town. It was rare to see a girl whose appearance made such a statement. A mixture of weird and wired, but it worked. She resembled a rock star, but instead of strumming an electric guitar, she was making music with a well-tuned superbike.

Out the door of Grant's and into the cold winter's air, the girl pulled her jacket's collar up around her neck and wheeled the Crusher past me—right under my nose. She reminded me of someone—of course, the reflection in the window. Suddenly, she stared into my eyes and beamed a five-alarm smile.

"Isn't she sublime?" the punkster spoke in a raspy voice with an English accent. When I scratched my head, she added: "It derives from Latin *sublimis,* meaning lofty or super fine."

I struggled to speak but could only spout mumbo jumbo. Clearly my brain wasn't firing on all cylinders. That's when I noticed her jeans were rolled up to the knee, exposing a pair of bright red stockings above laced-up boots. Interesting.

She broke the ice. "I'm Wahoo."

Wahoo? Was she serious? I stifled a laugh. "Hi, I'm Bart, but everyone calls me Bub."

"Kind of a funky name," she teased, her tongue peeking through grinning teeth.

Taken aback, I spurted out, "Wahoo's not exactly mainstream, you know." Touché.

This made her smile even more. "It was the first word from my mother's mouth after I was born," Wahoo said. "I guess the doc thought it was my name, because that's what he put on my birth certificate. It just stuck to me like superglue," she continued with a chuckle.

I nodded, unsure how to respond to this oddly cool girl. "So . . . where are you taking my, uh, the Crimson Crusher?" I asked, turning my attention back to the bike. Outside the shop now, in broad daylight, the blanket of snow reflected the sun's brilliant rays off the frame, making me squint.

I was snowed, pun intended.

"That way." Wahoo pointed vaguely. "I work for a Christmas catalog company—RSS, Inc. Maybe you've heard of it?"

"RSS? You work in that weird warehouse down the street?" Maybe she could explain the loud noises I'd heard.

"Weird warehouse?" She giggled. "I'll have to tell the Stocklings you called it that, Bub."

Whoa! This was getting stranger by the minute. "Stocklings? Wait, you didn't buy the Crusher for yourself?"

"No, no. I'm not much of a cyclist. Actually, I prefer sleighs and carriages," she said with a twinkle in her eye. "We're selling the bike at a special auction."

"Auction?" Maybe all hope wasn't lost. Didn't lots of crazy things happen at auctions? Maybe no other bidders would show, and I could snatch it up for a dollar. I would even wear my zombie Halloween outfit with fake blood to scare away bidders. My eyes lit up at the prospect.

"Yep. We'll put the bike on the block and raise as much as possible to help fund the other gifts."

Hmm. That last part didn't sound good. The bike's price could skyrocket even higher than $500—already unaffordable. Then I'd be kissing my coveted Crusher good-bye forever. No chance of summer bliss with friends. No chance of outriding Bugsy. And to be honest . . . no chance of showing off to the world.

My excellent day was starting to unravel.

"But why do you need to raise money to pay for gifts? Don't people buy them through your catalog?" I asked, pumping for more answers.

"RSS is a charitable Christmas catalog company, which is why I got a discount on the bike," Wahoo explained. "Starting with St. Nicholas, the original Santa in about 300 A.D., giving is what Christmas is all about. Children from around the world receive gifts from RSS."

I felt a burning sense of envy. Not that I wasn't happy for those kids, whoever they were, to get special gifts. But it was hard enough that our family would have a "scanty" Christmas, and now the perfect present was disappearing too. My Christmas spirit was tanking fast.

"Are you all right?" Wahoo asked, gazing into my eyes with concern. "You're white as whipped cream."

"I'm whipped, but it's okay," I mumbled, forcing myself to take a deep breath and focus. "When is this auction?" Maybe the Kitchen Kitty would miraculously triple in size before then.

"You really crave this bike, huh?" she said, eyeing the Crimson Crusher with newfound respect. "Why don't you come by for a visit? She'll be on display inside RSS for the next week with an auction just before Christmas. Just drop in to say hello . . . even place a bid."

That was a joke. As she swung her leg over and started mounting the Crusher, I realized I'd been too upset to delve further. And now she was leaving. "Wait, uh, Wahoo . . ." I still couldn't get over her name.

She paused, one foot still on a pedal. "Yep?"

"What exactly are Stocklings anyway?"

"Our nickname for special workers who help stock the shelves."

Well, that didn't reveal much. "Tell me one cool thing about Stocklings."

"They're always hungry!"

I left that one alone. "Do they make all that noise?"

"I don't know what you mean, Bub. Noise is all around, including your own heart—just listen for a thump."

"I've never heard one before."

"Not surprised. Well, keep on trying. Thumps are good for your health." Her eyes sparkled.

What wasn't she telling me? What were Stocklings doing in there? Could they be visiting aliens? I'd seen something like that on the Sci-Fi Channel. "If I come by the warehouse, can I check it all out?" I probed.

"Maybe, maybe not. Depends on your grit. See ya, sport!" Without waiting for my response, Wahoo handed me her glittering business card and took off on the Crusher. She clumsily cycled away like it was the first time riding a bike in her life. Did I hear her squeal "Wahoooo!" as she splashed through a slushy pothole?

As I watched her pedaling unevenly down the street, Wahoo's words echoed in my mind. What did she mean by the grit thing? Would I be eaten alive by the "hungry" Stocklings first? Did I have to bid on the bike to see what they were up to in that warehouse? No matter, since I had no cash to my name. I racked my brain. What if I won the lottery? Or wished on a falling star? Or found money on the street? All about as likely as the big guy in suspenders making it happen. I let out a long sigh. "Where's Mr. Claus when you need him?"

A swift, icy breeze nudged at the Santa with sleigh model suspended from a nearby billboard. It creaked loudly, as if answering, "Ho ho ho! Here I am!"

I shook my head. Not even close.

Realizing I'd not asked what RSS meant, I watched Wahoo's form recede and wondered if it related to her scarlet stockings. While most would have a "White Christmas" that year, I had a gut feeling mine would be colored by shades of red.

CHAPTER 3

I trudged through the fresh powder to our front porch, my boots plowing little valleys in the mountains of snow.

"Did you shovel the walk, Bub?" Dad asked as I slipped out of my coat and snow-caked boots. Ugh, I had forgotten . . . again.

"Not exactly," I said, still reeling from my hopeless day.

"Well, Bub, you know it's your job to—"

"I know, Dad," I snapped without thinking.

"Young man!" He raised his eyebrows and stared me down.

"Okay, sorry, I'm going," I conceded.

I donned my coat and shoved wet feet back into cold boots before stomping outside. As I grabbed the shovel and got to work, I couldn't get the Crusher out of my head. If I visited the warehouse, could I earn a bid? Maybe shovel their walks for pay? Ha, doubtful if I needed Dad as a reference. But mostly I thought about Wahoo, wondering what she and Stocklings actually did at RSS. She didn't look the type to lug around boxes. In fact, she could barely ride a bicycle in a straight line, so I found it hard to believe she drove a forklift to move heavy pallets, crates, and whatnot. She was obviously a big cheese, maybe a punk rock star or relative of the owner.

The front door creaked open, and Chad poked out his head. "Where'd you go earlier?"

"Out. Who are you, my mom?" I wasn't in the mood for chitchat.

"Where?"

"Okay, I'll answer one question." I set down the shovel. "I went to Grant's and"—I sighed—"they sold the best bike on the planet."

"Not the Blue Beast!"

"No! The Crimson Crusher, doofus. And believe it or not, a pink-haired lady punkster paid cash and bought her," I said, shoveling again. "It's the absolute story of my life, the worst thing *ever*."

"Oh," Chad said, now more sympathetic. "No wonder you're grumpy."

"I'm not grumpy!" I shouted, sounding very grumpy. "I'm just irritated 'cause now I've got nothing to look forward to."

"There's Christmas."

I knew Chad was trying to cheer me up, but forget it. "I meant something real to look forward to," I grumbled while hefting the last snow off the walk.

"Mom says Christmas is about family and religion and fun. Aren't those real?"

"Whatever," I said, waving him off, stomping into the house.

"What does that mean?" Chad muttered.

"It means you're ten!" I hollered back.

Chad shut the front door as Dad poked in his head from the kitchen. "Everything outside done, Bub?"

"Yes, sir."

"Thanks, son. Nice to see you earning pocket money by doing chores." Dad reached into his back pocket and extended a crumpled five-dollar bill—my weekly allowance. "Take this and run. In my day I only got—"

"I know, two dollars a week, times were tough." I fake-smiled politely as I took the measly fiver that would maybe buy four chocolate clusters at Candy Confection or two Happy Meals at Mickey D's. Running on empty, I headed, eyes downcast, to the kitchen.

"Don't spend it all in one place. Well, let me grab another tool," Dad said as he hobbled back to his garage workshop, leaving me to mischief.

I hadn't planned to peek, really; I just wanted a protein snack, but curiosity spurred me on. Checking that the coast was clear, I quietly crept over the jumbled tool box in the kitchen and ignored the nest of wires protruding from our relic toaster. Mister Fix It, my handy dad, was on the rampage again.

Slowly, slowly, I slid open the counter drawer and withdrew the Kitchen Kitty. Lifting off the top, I took a deep breath and checked inside, counting only $300 in reserve.

"Nuts," I murmured. It was hardly a rich treasure chest. Suddenly, I wasn't hungry anymore.

Climbing the stairs two at a time, I stormed into my bedroom and threw myself outstretched onto bed, staring at the ceiling. There had to be some way to earn my ticket to biker's paradise. I needed to chill awhile and think.

In my lousy state of mind, I was ill prepared for what followed.

"Are ya busy, Bub?" Chad asked, entering hesitantly.

"Yes!" I blurted out while adjusting my horror film posters covering one wall. Now Chad was standing in my room. Why was he in my room? "You want something?"

Chad rubbed his elbow and bit his lip. "I just asked Dad if Santa was real or a hoax?"

I sighed, feeling responsible after our little spat. "And what did Dad say?"

"He sidestepped it—the usual tactics. He said: 'Santa's real, but only if you believe in him,'" Chad answered with a pout, doing his best Dad voice. "What he and Mom always say."

I hesitated, weighing my options. This was a pivotal moment in Chad's life and mine; I didn't want to emotionally scar him into being a fruitcake or serial killer or hate me forever. I took the easy way out and answered, "Sounds reasonable to me."

Not convincing.

"C'mon, Bub, tell me the truth, bro to bro," Chad urged, plopping down on the foot of my bed. "I'm not going anywhere."

"Um, okay."

"All my friends say he's fake, and since I'm on Honor Roll, I'm smart enough to know that."

"You are the brainiac," I agreed, recalling shelves of science books in his bedroom versus comics and action figures in mine. Lots of questions about life and the universe . . . brilliant. If he'd been at all interested in RSS, Inc., its mystery would've been solved in a flash.

I didn't want to pop his balloon filled with rare air.

"Mom says you and I are both smart, but in different ways. I have more book sense, but you're cleverer. Street smart. You're not—"

"Naïve?"

Chad nodded. "I guess. Well, we both have big imaginations, so together we'll figure it out, huh?"

"Uh . . . figure out what exactly?"

"The truth. Tell me, is Santa real? I need to know."

I sighed and stroked my chin while staring into his eyes—full of hope and wonder. "I don't know, Chad. I mean, I don't spend time thinking if legends are real or not. Take Big Foot, Loch Ness Monster, Santa —are they real? And what exactly is real, anyway? It's a tough question—"

"You're stalling!" Chad accused. "You sound like a politician."

"Everyone has to figure it out for himself," I continued, touching his shoulder. "You love reading science, right? How do you think Santa can deliver millions of presents worldwide, in one night, and drop down so many hot chimneys without getting barbecued? Plus he'd need his stomach pumped after all the cookies and pepto. Even Superman would upchuck that load."

"I know it doesn't make sense. But Mom and Dad always answer that it's Santa magic."

"There you go," I replied enthusiastically, relieved that explaining this age-old myth was off my shoulders.

"Is there real magic, Bub? Please, tell me, I gotta know," Chad continued, leaning forward.

I had to put this gently, not wanting to kill his Christmas spirit just because I wasn't getting my Crusher. "Chad, we see things in varying ways at different ages. I'm older than you, so my opinion might not be the same as yours."

"I thought my big brother'd have the glory guts to tell me the truth," he said bitterly.

"Unfair! I've got buckets of glory guts, whatever that is."

"Gross. Look, I'm not stupid, Bub. I know about fake Santas—like in the movies, actors play the part of Santa, not really him. And those guys with cotton beards and goat breath who stand in for him at Clarke's every year—I know they're not real either. Mom says they take Santa's place while he's getting in shape for Christmas Eve. Is that true?" Chad pressed.

"It is, sort of . . . but just leave it alone, Chad. It'll all work out as you grow up, okay?" I said, trying not to get frustrated. "Hey, it's actually profitable to believe. More loot, ha!"

"Why can't I get a straight answer?" Chad shouted. He stood and trudged toward the door before turning back and staring through me. "Okay, I'll ask a different question. One day when I'm almost twelve years old, like you, what will I think about Santa magic? Don't worry, I can handle anything you say if it's true."

Fine!

He'd asked for it. "Okay, you want the absolute truth? It's *not* what you think it is."

Chad's face turned deep red—that color again—and cracked into a painful frown. "Oh, no!" He yelped like a scalded dog, sobbing as he raced out the door before I could say another word.

Then I heard him stomping around in his room followed by

scuffling and thuds. Next, a big wallop as he slammed shut his bedroom door. I stuck my head out to check if the house was still standing. From his book shelves, Chad had grabbed favorite holiday classics, from *The Night Before Christmas* to *The Polar Express*, and tossed them like garbage in a heap outside his door.

I felt rotten, but there was nothing more I could do. His bubble had burst. "Welcome to the club," I muttered to myself. Maybe it was best that Chad learned early on that he was wasting his time. But deep down, I knew I'd totally shocked him. And I had no idea how to reverse it. In fact, I wished I could have hit reset to rekindle the Santa fire inside of me too. Chad had kept the last embers of hope burning a long while, even if it irked me sometimes. The truth was, now the house would seem less joyous without his happy face lighting up our holidays every waking moment.

"What's going on here?" Mom asked, looking drained as she climbed the stairs to find the discarded pile of books.

She had changed uniforms and was wearing a blue apron from her shift at Vel's Florist Shop in town. Taking in a deep breath, I had to admit the fresh scent of flowers sure beat the smell of onion soup.

"I've been pricked by so many holly sprigs—my fingers are like Swiss cheese," she noted, holding up her hands. "Now, Bub, can you explain why Chad emptied the shelves of his entire Christmas collection? He loves Christmas."

"He did love it," I said bluntly.

"Oh, Bub. What did you do?"

"Nothing!"

"Tell me more, young man," Mom insisted.

I leaped to my own defense. "Okay, he asked if Santa Claus was real. He wanted the truth, and I said, 'It's not what you think it is'—that's all."

"Bub!" Mom said, shaking her head. She bent over and started picking up the books, cradling them in her arms.

"Sorry, I'm sure he'll get over it. I mean, I did . . . well, mostly." I picked up the last book and placed it atop the others. "Where are you taking them?"

"Somewhere safe until he appreciates them again," she replied, heading off to the master bedroom, carrying the once treasured tomes. "This is a sad day. Disillusionment hurts."

I couldn't help following her. Mom opened an old sweater box and placed Chad's holiday classics neatly inside. As she wiped a tear from her cheek, I slipped away unseen.

Mom was another casualty of my horrible day. At this rate, a lump of coal was exactly what I deserved in my Christmas stocking. Back in my room, stomach churning, I sprawled across the bed and gathered my thoughts. . . .

It felt like I was on the *Titanic*, full speed ahead, without a lifeboat. Maybe it was time to turn things around, to restore some hope to all this Bah-humbug, to become a lot less Scrooge and a little more Tiny Tim. To take matters into my own hands and face the consequences.

And I knew exactly where to start: mysterious RSS, Inc.

CHAPTER 4

I shivered standing in front of the entrance to RSS, Inc., but not from the cold. The door was covered in a layer of jet-black paint and adorned with an oddly ornate brass knocker, shaped like the head of an antler-less moose. It looked like something on the front door of a haunted house—as if it might open its mouth suddenly, drag my hand inside, and spit out the bones. Since there was no doorbell, I just needed to build up the nerve to knock.

I can do this, I thought. But as I reached for the knocker, that noise erupted again. I stopped in my tracks. The clunking, grinding sound was echoing from behind the door!

I dared to slowly lean forward and place my ear against the wood. Holding my breath, I listened closely. There was something mechanical happening. Something big was moving around, possibly dragging its feet . . . or a tail? Yes, it sounded like a robotic dragon was skulking in the warehouse, rather than machinery I'd heard before.

Then the clunky sounds ended abruptly, only to be replaced by the creak of a sliding bolt and heavy grinding twist and click of an old lock. The door was opening. I leaped backward and just stood there with my mouth wide open. If the snout of some metallic beast had appeared, I was primed to run like the wind.

"Splendiferous, Bub, thought you'd be stopping by," sang the familiar voice of Wahoo. She appeared unfazed, without a pink hair out of place, to find me standing there on the doorstep.

"I never knocked. How'd you know I was here?" I asked, looking around for cameras—none.

"It's my job," Wahoo answered. "Before entering, beware the Snorking Bandersnitch who's a bit of a chocolate thief." Her jabberwocky rendered me speechless. She held up a weathered mat with the words *Welcome, Bienvenue, Willkommen,* and so on, written in many languages. "I was about to roll out the magic you-know-what," she said with a grin, tossing the red-and-black mat at my feet. "This carpet's had loads of traffic: big feet, small feet, dirty feet. You're one of the above. And I run a tight ship, mate—wipe 'em clean or walk the plank!" she deadpanned.

Wahoo turned to amble back inside. I found myself shuffling across the mat behind her, impatient to explore, groping to say something intelligent. The door slammed shut with a boom and click, and I spun around to observe a heavy spring hinge.

"Wow, built like a fortress," I remarked.

"Don't worry," Wahoo said, placing a reassuring hand on my shoulder. "This place takes care of itself—hard to enter but easy to leave. Almost like it has a mind of its own."

"This place . . . what is it?" I inquired, feeling uneasy, checking out the confines of the shadowy corridor as we continued walking.

"In its day, a flagship Macy's Department Store. But, my

boss—Mr. Mabrey—made, shall we say, major modifications. He's a mechanical marvel. Now it runs like a well-oiled machine."

"Machine?" I felt warmer and warmer with every step taken, so I pulled off my hat. "Now that you mention it, that explains those grinding noises."

Wahoo flicked me a teasing glance. "Well, what else would you expect from our—as you say—weird warehouse, huh, Bub?"

"Right. Um, where are we going?" The corridor seemed to be getting narrower and narrower, bottlenecking at a short door barely wide enough for a child to fit through.

"Not much farther," Wahoo replied. "Hope you're not claustrophobic; it's kind of a squeeze."

It was the wackiest thing I'd seen so far. A small door to enter a huge warehouse. "How'd you get the Crimson Crusher through here?" I asked while cramming into the doorway.

"Oh, I took her around the back, through the warehouse entrance. Only visitors and most Stocklings use this door. Keep pushing—squeezing's therapeutic except with hungry pythons."

I chuckled and popped through the doorframe. If my experience so far was the norm, Wahoo would keep me on my toes. "Are Stocklings related to Munchkins by any chance?"

"Funny you should ask. When Mr. Mabrey designed the door, most Stocklings were able to fit through it easily—some were like Munchkins. Now our applicants are taller, more average-size folks, with bigger appetites. And Mr. Mabrey hadn't really planned on RSS receiving many outside visitors—we're highly selective. You're the first we've had in some time."

"Hope that's good for everyone," I said, recalling that Munchkins were fantasy folks.

I let out a gasp as I stood fully upright and absorbed the incredible sight of the warehouse's cavernous interior. The ceiling was blanketed in a net of sparkling fairy lights, like a starlit sky, illuminating ten towering units, each housing shelves and more shelves, laden with every toy, game, book, and gizmo imaginable. I was amazed by the wonder of it all—a feast of delights for young and old. Holographic hula hoops spun on hooks at the end of each row, while Animatronic singing monkeys performed gymnastics on dancing trees. Tiny robots whirred during a game of floor hockey with flashing pucks at lightning speed. A miniature train whistled and belched red smoke as it defied gravity by riding up walls and across ceilings! And I could hardly believe the dollhouses with LED panels and sound effects, changing scenery, and automated figures.

At the opposite end of the room was a spacious, glass-walled office. Sitting behind his mahogany desk was a portly gentleman with rosy cheeks and a jovial smile peeking through a full, white beard. He was studiously reading a book, and if not dressed in a white shirt and tie instead of a red suit, could've been a dead ringer for Santa himself. Above the door was a simple sign: *Roy Mabrey, CEO & Chief Bottle Washer*.

"Your boss looks like a cross between two childhood myths: Paul Bunyan and Santa Claus," I commented, trying to impress Wahoo.

She paused before nodding. "Yep, others have noted the Santa resemblance as well."

And why not, since Christmas seemed to be what RSS was all about anyway.

Amid the hustle and bustle of the warehouse, I caught sight of my Crusher—shiny as ever—parked in the center of the floor!

"The Stocklings have been polishing her, ready for the big auction," Wahoo said proudly, admiring the handsome bike. "They cleaned off the splatters and splotches from my ride over here. Think I found every slushy puddle in town."

I took a few steps and circled the Crusher before spotting a handwritten tag. "$600—is that the going price?"

"Yep. That's the opening bid—should be a hot auction."

"Sure . . . hot auction," I muttered, my dreams evaporating fast.

"You seem distressed. Talk to me, Bub."

"Well," I replied, my voice cracking, "that tag might as well say six million 'cause it's way out of my league." I swallowed and cleared my throat—embarrassed. "My pocket money is only five bucks a week, so I could come back and bid in about ten years?"

Wahoo looked concerned. "If you'd like to bid on this item, could you raise the money before Christmas?"

"You mean like a job? Well, there are paper routes, but my bike is too beat-up for that. So, unless you're hiring . . ." I said, holding back a lump in my throat.

"I'm in charge of Human Resources—actually I am Human

Resources," Wahoo declared. "What's your experience, young man? Boast or you're toast."

Was she teasing me again? Yet the look in her eyes was sincere. "Um, well . . ." I racked my brain for an answer, clueless about job interviews. "I snow shovel for pay, and my science project on bats won second. And . . ." I glanced around, grasping for straws, noticing her legs. "Stockings . . . your sign on the roof. I've sold lemonade, so I could sell stockings for you, up and down Main." Since most of that was lame, I added: "My parents say I have wit and courage."

Wahoo nodded. "Thanks for coming; I'm also fascinated by nocturnal creatures like bats."

I looked down, defeated until—

"How could I pass up those credentials? You're hired!" Wahoo affirmed with a smile.

"Seriously?" Was I even old enough for a real job? This was a far cry from shoveling our front walk. Maybe she was joking. "You want me to work at RSS at my age?"

Wahoo nodded. "We need all hands on deck running up to the holidays—our busiest time of the year," she explained. "So, I can offer you one hundred per week, working here in our Wish Fulfillment Center, starting tomorrow. What say ye?"

"I'll take it and run. Thanks!" I didn't know what to do next. Should I shake her hand off? Give her a hug? High-five? None of those felt right. "So, does this make me a Stockling?"

Chuckling, she answered: "Not quite. Let's call you a Stockling Hire In Training."

Suddenly, I realized that, besides Wahoo and Mr. Mabrey, no other workers were in sight. I craned my neck to look around. "Where are they anyway?"

"On Choc-Nog break. We always stop midmorning for chocolate milk, hot chocolate, or eggnog—best in the universe. One of the perks of working here."

Was she serious or delirious?

Choosing the former, I relaxed. The idea of working at a place that offered free chocolate drinks was invigorating. That thought was interrupted by a shrill whistle that filled every corner of the warehouse. I cupped my ears until it stopped.

"Break's over. Here they come," Wahoo said as a small side door opened. A diverse-looking group of people—Stocklings, I guessed—wandered out, wiping eggnog and chocolate from mouths onto sleeves. Someone belched, eliciting giggles.

Each guy or girl, of all different ages, was wearing the same uniform of red shirt and green pants—rolled up to the knee to reveal a pair of stockings. Some wore a pair of red stockings, while others had one red and one black. "Wahoo, why the different-colored stockings? Does it mean something?"

"Kind of a ranking system . . . for those who qualify. Wearing the other garb is voluntary."

"Oh, so you have two red stockings since you're a supervisor?"

"Something like that," she said cryptically.

"Do stockings relate to the name RSS?" I asked, tuning in more since I was an employee.

"Very good, Bub. Welcome to the Red Stocking Society, local

facility; we have branches all over the world including frigid places. Membership must be earned and isn't easy. If you dare to join us, you won't be sorry. I left Cambridge to come here and have never looked back."

Before I could digest her comments, I heard that grinding, thudding sound again. Only it was much louder coming from inside, like a freight train thundering past.

I swiveled my head to locate the origin of the noise. One Stockling, a sinewy teenage guy wearing sunglasses, was cranking a large wheel with a handle. When the wheel turned, so did a series of cogs along the wall. Then a tremendous grating noise erupted from below a big shelving unit as it inched forth, scraping the stone floor.

Mystery solved.

As if moved by a magical force, the enormous shelving unit, loaded with a bounty of toys and gifts, rotated 180 degrees on the spot. I watched in awe, dust stirring up around the unit, as the grating and grinding reached a fever pitch. The entire unit had turned completely around to reveal a flip side of shelves loaded with more toys and boxes!

Total silence when the shelving unit stopped moving. The Stockling wearing shades left his post on the wheel crank and felt carefully along the shelf, as if blindly exploring with his hands. Smoothing his fingers over the fur of a plush teddy bear, he smiled and plucked it from the shelf. Next, he navigated to a wrapping station while counting his steps, lowered the bear into the exact-size cardboard box, and reached for a roll of silver paper.

All in a day's work as a Stockling.

"See you soon, Bub," Wahoo said, snapping me out of my trance. "Get your parents' permission for the job and report back here at 9 a.m. sharp." She glanced over her shoulder at the Stocklings. "I'd better get back to work. You can let yourself out," she concluded and stepped away to chat with two merry Stocklings who were poring over a list on a clipboard. But were they checking it twice?

"Right. Uh, see you later," I murmured as I backtracked toward the small door to the corridor, still taking in the immense room. It was suddenly a beehive of activity as Stocklings rushed around with packages in their arms. No one paid much attention to me, until someone tapped on my shoulder. I spun around to realize I was standing in the path of a very serious girl my age.

"You're blocking me," she said impatiently and blew right past me.

Flustered, I mumbled an apology and moved on, all the while observing the Stocklings' joint effort. Teamwork had never been my bag. Would I or could I fit in with them?

As the small door clicked shut, I started treading down the barely lit corridor toward the entrance. Suddenly, flickering shadows seemed to be chasing me, and I was bursting to get back into the light of day! I pulled down my hat and zipped my coat tighter, already feeling the cold air whistling through cracks around the front door. Then something caught my eye. When I'd entered earlier, that opening didn't exist—a deep passageway off the corridor.

No way I could have missed it. Cautiously, I stepped toward it, my curiosity at war with my nerves.

In the dim light, barely visible, was a twisting tunnel with offshoots—a virtual maze of chambers in near-pitch darkness. I strained to see past the veil of shadows and shivered in my boots. That spooky sense again—like being watched—but I couldn't detect anyone else. What was it that Wahoo had said about nocturnal creatures?

"H-Hello?" I stammered. Silence. Unsure whether to be disappointed or relieved, I chose not to hang around to investigate.

No way, José.

Cheetah fast, I shot through the door into chilly sunlight, a welcome shock to the system. Incredibly, I'd just visited an impressive toy factory where I was actually going to work. Now my prized Crusher wasn't quite as far out of reach.

But the lingering feeling that RSS was much more than it seemed, something boiling under the surface, stuck with me. And if my job there was a good thing, why did I feel more secure outside than inside those walls?

CHAPTER 5

That night, I was haunted by vivid nightmares of crawling on my hands and knees down the dark, narrow corridor in the warehouse, feeling every dusty, grimy inch with my fingertips. As I ran my hands over rough cracks and bumps on the uneven flooring, inching toward that narrow door, I feared what might lie in wait.

Eerie cranking, grinding, and crunching noises echoed in the tunnel, louder and louder . . . until finally, the door abruptly opened, bathing me in light.

A monstrous, growling Bugsy—evil grin with fangs bared—awaited me!

"Morning, sunshine," greeted Mom, flinging open the curtains. "Another wild dream? You need to cut down on chocolate."

"No, I need more chocolate. What time is it?" I croaked, my heart drumming.

"Past eight," she replied.

"Oh, no! I'll be late my first day of work!" I yelled, dashing from my room, almost barging into Dad.

"First day where?" Dad asked, bemused.

"First day at my new job. Mom said it was okay. Tell you 'bout it later," I called out, glancing back at him. I even waved, unlike my usual style.

Awakened by the ruckus, Chad opened his door and sighed before slamming it shut—not a happy camper.

Dad was left scratching his head—the only unemployed person left in the house. Even Chad had managed to charm some elderly neighbors into hiring him for snow removal. Normally he'd be dreaming about gifts under the tree and helping prep for the big day, but after our talk he'd decided to pursue his own gifts. I felt regretful over deflating him, but at least he was trying to be positive.

Gobbling a chocolate cluster for energy, I got ready in a flash and booked it down to RSS, Inc., dragging my heels the last few steps to the front door. I couldn't shake off my nightmare of that creepy corridor and horrible ending.

"C'mon, I'm growing a beard—we'll be late!" a voice spoke behind me. I spun around to see the fellow with sunglasses who'd been cranking shelves the day before. And now I noticed he was holding a white cane, tapping it against my shoes, which were blocking his path. "Wahoo won't be pleased if we're late."

"Wahoo not happy? I can't imagine it," I remarked. She seemed the type of person who was always golden.

"My name's Jett," the Stockling announced, gently pushing past me.

"I'm Bub," I replied, now aware he was blind.

Jett approached the front door and reached up to the knocker, grasping it firmly with one hand. With a quick twist, the head turned to the right and unlocked the door. I knew there was something odd about that knocker.

"How many secrets does this place hold?" I asked in amazement.

"I've lost count," Jett said with a smile. "C'mon, we'd better hustle."

I followed Jett inside the dark corridor that was even narrower than I recalled. As we moved past the passageway leading to a labyrinth of tunnels, I peered down it to see if anyone or thing was lurking. Instantly, there was a crack of red light beneath a stone wall, gone in the blink of an eye. "Did you see that?" I asked before I could stop myself.

"No, but I heard a shuffle," Jett said coolly. "Not unusual, maybe a mouse scareder than you. Rumor has it a phantom psychopath roams RSS chewing on exposed ears. Boo!" He grinned.

Gulping, I walked behind him until we reached the small door. Barely squeezing through, we emerged into the warehouse area, where Wahoo was impatiently tapping her shoe. "Morning, gents. Bub, you look more like you do today than you did yesterday."

"Thanks. Huh?"

"Lost time is never found again," she quipped, frowning. "You two are one minute late."

"Sorry, I—" But before I could voice my flimsy excuse, she cracked a smile.

"Don't sweat it, Bub. As long as everything is ready for Christmas Eve delivery, there's no such thing as late around here."

Stepping forward, she whispered in my ear: "Just don't let it happen again or you could be castigated."

What?

I had no clue the word meant to scold or reprimand, but I was never late again. Meanwhile, Jett had disappeared without me even noticing his stocking status. Those pesky stockings were planted in my mind.

Wahoo whistled loudly to gather the troops. "All Coreys breathing . . . gather 'round. Something conferential."

"Let me introduce you to the rest of the team," Wahoo said as I hung up my jacket.

As we strolled toward the break room, I had to ask, "Is that where they, uh, feed?"

Wahoo raised an eyebrow. "Yep, there's feeding going on in there. They love snacking on finger foods; be careful with yours."

Hands firmly in my pockets, I followed Wahoo inside where the Stocklings were munching on appetizers. The gang relaxed around a table with feet up, each wearing one red and one black stocking. All except Jett promptly sat up straight and planted legs firmly on the floor. "Morning, Wahoo!" greeted a boy in a wheelchair as he nudged Jett to lower his feet too.

Jett quickly complied with a toothy grin in Wahoo's direction.

The break room, at least, looked fairly ordinary. There were a few cafeteria-style tables and chairs, black-and-white Christmas photos on the walls, a large refrigerator, and a countertop with sink, stovetop, microwave, and some sort of metal contraption.

Wahoo cleared her throat to address the group: "Morning, all . . . this is Bub, our next victim."

Memories of my nightmare danced before my eyes. I didn't know whether to dine or dash. All three Stocklings chuckled as I kept one eye on the exit.

Wahoo continued: "Seriously, Bub, I welcome you as a trainee for the core group that handles most up-front duties: gift retrieval and wrapping, marketing, computers. Each member is called a Corey."

"Rhymes with 'glory' since we bask in it," added Jett with thumbs-up.

I laughed and nodded. "There are four Coreys—or three and a half, since I'm just in training," I noted. "How about the other workers I saw yesterday?"

Wahoo resumed: "Thought you'd never ask! We have five Hivers: all busy bees in charge of toy-making, plus mailing, delivery, and odd jobs. There are also six Fixers who troubleshoot and handle maintenance, repair, and security. I've been lucky to serve in all three groups. Now let's welcome Bub the rookie and intro yourselves, Coreys."

The boy in the wheelchair nodded to me. "Hi, I think you've met Jett already. I'm Austin, and this is Kip." He pointed to the girl beside him—the one I'd blocked the day before. She weakly raised a hand to wave hello. "She's shy, sometimes," Austin added. Frowning, Kip poked him with a sharp elbow and stared at the wall.

Austin had raven hair that matched the leather seat of his

41

wheelchair. Everything about his chair was slick—custom green handles, sporty tires, and sparkling chrome. I could tell he'd been the one caring for my Crimson Crusher. "Nice wheels," I noted, admiring his handiwork.

"Thanks. I polish it every day, supernova bright," Austin boasted proudly.

Suddenly a cuckoo alarm sounded thrice, prompting Wahoo to say: "Three cuckoos—the mechanical wing again. Bub, you and Kip stay here; we'll go assist the Fixers." She and the other Stocklings hustled out, leaving Kip and me alone.

Which I didn't really mind.

"Hey, I'm Bart, but my nickname is Bub," I said, trying to catch Kip's eye. She was easy to look at, with chestnut-colored hair, cherry cheeks, and a cute pug nose. Her eyes were directed downward while chewing her lip.

Silence stretched across the room. Should I make conversation or something? Is that what grown-ups did in these situations? But what to say to a sharp girl who makes your knees weak? "Uh . . . I've always wondered, does lipstick taste like candy?" I asked, before realizing my stupidity. No response, lucky for me, because something else attracted her attention.

Following her line of sight, I saw a puppy—barely eight inches long—emerge from a backpack on the floor. The weirdest thing: He had on a doggy diaper and wore tiny, red, argyle stockings on all four legs. Kip's smile lit up the room as she scooped him up.

"Is he yours?" I asked. She nodded and put a finger to her lips; I got the message to keep it private. I stepped forward and petted his tiny head. His ears were twice as big as his face, which made him resemble a cute bat dog. Right up my alley. "Does he have a name?"

"Hercules," she stated proudly as the dog's ears perked up. She scratched behind his ears but didn't say more.

"Uh, where'd you buy those tiny stockings?" I asked, drawn to her gardenia scent.

"I knitted 'em—two weeks nonstop," she whispered. "I lived on vitamins and cabbage."

Kip was strange, but nice . . . similar to RSS, Inc., so far.

We heard the shuffle of footsteps outside the door, and Kip hid Hercules away before the others slipped back into the break room.

"A transverse decapacitator fizzled on the Robotic Elf Assembler," Wahoo announced, holding a Wingman multi-tool. "One new turbo fuse, a swift kick, and it's working like a charm now." She tapped my arm and pointed to the odd-looking countertop machine—a metal box with multiple levers and buttons, topped with a small chimney of sorts. "Thirsty?" she asked, as if directing me to a normal vending machine and not Willy Wonka's cappuccino maker.

The buttons were marked with pictograms instead of words. "Picture of the white cow means milk; brown cow is chocolate milk; steaming cow is hot cocoa; and yellow chicken is—"

"Eggnog?"

"You learn fast, rookie, and that's no yolk." Wahoo smiled at her own pun. "Have a go."

"How does it work?"

"Just tap the button; let it do the rest." She winked at me, one of those you-know-what-I-mean winks.

I certainly didn't know what she meant, but I suspected it would be something out of the ordinary.

"Uh, okay." I tapped the brown cow button and waited patiently for a cup to pop out of somewhere and fill with liquid. Gurgle! Glug! Hiss! Then, nothing. I glanced at Wahoo and the grinning faces of the Stocklings, who seemed to be waiting too. Was I being pranked? "I think it's broken."

"No, it's coming," Wahoo said, straight-faced. "Just smile like you're robbing a bank."

Suddenly, the Stocklings moved a step sideways.

I turned back to the machine and saw a tiny brown bubble building at the tip of a nozzle. "But there's no cup."

Before I could finish my thought, the nozzle let rip with a long stream of frothy chocolate milk, aimed smack-dab in the center of my face! At first it was painful, being slapped on my already cold nose with icy liquid. That is, until I smiled wide and swallowed a mouthful of the rich drink—sublime, the best I'd ever guzzled.

Hearing bubbles rush past my ears was like falling into a waterfall and being carried away by the current. When the blast from the nozzle subsided, I was left dripping and content. Milk in my hair, on my nose and cheeks, dribbling into my ears—even a puddle of chocolate milk on my shirt. All delicious. The Stocklings began clapping.

"Look at him—does he need a towel or a straw?" Austin chortled.

I glanced down and couldn't help myself—licking the puddle of chocolate milk right off my sleeve. As Wahoo cracked up, Jett snorted, and even Kip had to grin.

Almost rolling in the aisle, Wahoo added, "Anticipate deflatulation."

"What's that?" I asked.

"Rhymes with your real name. Look it up, Bub," she said playfully.

Jett patted me on the back apologetically, while Kip mustered a laugh. "Don't worry, Bub. It happens to the best of us," Jett said. "My first day the eggnog filled my boots, and two alley cats chased me home!"

Wahoo added: "Consider that an informal initiation, Bub. And next time, remember to stand back and open wide. The Drink-o-nator was designed by Mr. Mabrey and is precise at hitting its target. Designed to aim at tonsils, for best results. If yours are gone, good luck." She handed me a towel to dry off. "Don't worry though—for hot cocoa, you get a cup."

"It's incredible," I admitted, licking a rogue chocolate drop off my chin. I couldn't resist adding: "I'll bet the Bandersnitch loves this machine, huh? Best invention since the wheel."

"Absolutely, he drains it dry," Wahoo said, tongue in cheek, before ushering me from the break room. "Come on, lots more to see. And these guys need to get back to the grindstone. Mush, mush!"

The Stocklings hopped to it and followed Wahoo and me back into the warehouse area.

Nothing could surprise me now.

When out of their earshot, I had to ask Wahoo: "Uh, sort of a sensitive question, but do most of the workers here have special needs, starting with the Coreys? Just curious."

"Don't we all have special needs, Bub? You're special too; now let's move on." End of chat.

Rounding a corner, we found Austin wheeled up to a desk with an LED mega-screen above a supercomputer. He sat at the control panel, a modern marvel of touch screens and keypads. Lots of cool but also surprising, considering all of the low-tech stuff in the warehouse. Even the crazy drink-shooting dispenser could have been a steam-engine-powered contraption from the Wild Wild West. And most RSS equipment so far included ingenious cranks and cogs and wheels, accompanied by sound effects. A fascinating hodgepodge of old and new.

"Hi, guys," Austin greeted without looking up. He was speed typing into an apparent database of names and gifts.

"Austin's our tech wiz, graduated MIT at thirteen," Wahoo announced.

"Twelve," Austin corrected. "The night before my birthday. It's an irrelevant factoid except for bragging rights."

"Sorry, I was rounding off. Can you tell Bub what you're doing?" Wahoo asked.

Austin pointed to a stack of handwritten letters, one onscreen reading: *Santa, I luv u, Red Dude.* "I'm scanning the 'Dear Santa' letters into a program using Passmore's formal verification logic that sorts 'wishes' into database fields, matching the right gifts with the right kids."

My eyes widened. "Like a tekkie version of Santa? Making kids' wishes come true?"

Wahoo beamed proudly. "Yep, we do try to channel Santa Claus—it's the charitable part of the business, giving Christmas presents to deserving kids."

"But," I wondered aloud, "who decides who is 'deserving'?"

Wahoo gazed over her shoulder at the glass-walled office of Mr. Mabrey. "Ultimately, the owner of RSS—Mr. Roy Mabrey," Wahoo disclosed. "After his brother—who dearly loved Christmas—disappeared a few years back, he decided to dedicate his fortune in memoriam to keeping the Santa spirit alive. He knows how tough it is to wish for something with all your heart and not receive it. Providing gifts and fulfilling wishes for kids was the only thing that returned a smile to his face."

I took a long peek at Mr. Mabrey's office. Smiling from ear to ear, he had his feet up on the desk and was talking expressively into a land line. The man looked jolly enough, but maybe this was one of his good days.

"Mr. Mabrey has final say on which kids deserve a charitable gift if the computer algorithm has an unresolved result," Austin chimed in. "He has an instinct for what's real need versus greed."

"An algo-what-em?" I asked, completely lost.

"An algorithm . . . like a formula to calculate who's been naughty and who's been nice," Austin replied matter-of-factly.

"Naughty and nice?" This was going from high tech to ridiculous really fast. "I mean, how could you tell that from a letter?"

"Easy. The program studies all wishes and personal info that the kids share, even analyzing synchronic linguistics and graphology, uh, handwriting, to see if they're being truthful."

My head was starting to spin, maybe also due to the chill of milk in my damp hair.

"The result is our master list," Wahoo elaborated, nodding toward a printer that was feeding a stream of paper piling up on the floor. "We also have a 3-D Proplastonic Printer that can produce almost any solid toy imaginable."

"Wow, I'm totally confused but totally awed at the same time."

Austin chuckled. "You'll get the hang of this place eventually. It monitors us 24/7 to make sure things run smoothly."

It?

For the second time, I looked up, checking for hidden cameras. Was the computer watching all the Stocklings? Or was the building itself keeping us locked in and on task? This entire place, supercomputer included, was equal parts creepy and cool.

Too much to process in one day.

My pondering was interrupted by a clunky sigh from a mobile shelving unit out in the main warehouse. I peered around the corner, where Jett was cranking the handle.

Unexpectedly, there she was again!

Two banks of shelves slid back, parting in unison to reveal the jaw-dropping Crimson Crusher. Still calling my name with her sparkling frame . . . primed to take on the world.

Wahoo nudged me in the ribs. "Enough ogling, Bub. Time to earn your keep. We'll start you off slowly at this level before you need to move at warp speed. Have fun."

I nodded and smiled sheepishly as she walked away, while the crunching noise surged even louder. Beyond that, in a distant corner of the vast room, I caught a distinct flash of *red* that quickly melted into the shadows.

Overactive imagination? Sleep deprivation? Chocolate overload? Not this time.

Now I was certain of it: In addition to Wahoo, Mr. Mabrey, and the Stocklings, something else roamed the RSS warehouse. Something beyond the chocolate-craving "Bandersnitch" that Wahoo and I had joked about. At least I thought it was a joke.

And this person—or Red Phantom—had *me* directly in its sights.

CHAPTER 6

My fellow Coreys made me feel welcome—or at least, less awkward—while teaching me the ropes as time marched on before Christmas. But the learning curve was Rocky Mountain steep.

I still hadn't figured out what the stockings were all about, and even kindly Kip was mum about it. Worse, seemingly every gizmo required a special knack or trick to make it perform its task. I found this out one day when simply pressing the Down button to take the elevator to the basement. . . .

After waiting five minutes, scratching my head, Wahoo appeared on the scene. "Down is up," she said.

"Excuse me?"

She had stopped to enjoy the show. "We're already in the basement, don't you know?" she teased. "Up takes you to the level above, where we store inventory before sorting it onto our shelves—down here," she added with a sneaky smile.

Still confused, I half-heartedly pressed the Up button. Within seconds, the elevator doors magically opened. "How can this be the basement when we're at street level?"

"Are we, Bub? Think about it—no windows in the main

warehouse area, but the outside of the building is covered with them."

Of course, I should have clued in when I saw the dimly lit main floor, illuminated mostly by fairy lights and oil lamps. "But how is that possible?"

Wahoo spelled it out. "When you enter the front and go down that narrow corridor, you're literally going down. It's a subtle slope that leads into this lower level basement. The opposite occurs when you exit the back at ground level. It's built that way to help logistics."

"So, I've been working down below all this time?" I noted, in awe again. "No wonder I blink like Mole Man when I leave at the end of the day."

"You'll get accustomed. Remember there are places like the North Pole, where Inuits live in darkness for half the year," Wahoo said, continuing on her way. "Doors are closing. Be safe."

I glanced back to see the elevator shutting automatically. With a jerk, I leaped forward and thrust my arm inside, just in time. The doors recoiled as I entered to select the button for Inventory that was amazingly above me.

The single-floor trip seemed longer than expected and was accompanied by loud clanks and clunks, like I was inside the warehouse core. It was my first task in Inventory—time to shine.

The doors finally opened to reveal another dark space, despite the banks of windows on all sides. Towering rows of boxes blocked much of the daylight, casting the room in shadows that protected stock from the heat and sunrays.

I gaped at the massive inventory and checked the printed list from Austin, who'd given me only a penlight for the job . . . sort of a test. My task was to retrieve a box of Laughing Lola dolls, the hot property on little girls' wish lists. I'd keep this private, as I cringed at the idea of buddies or Chad knowing I was hauling around girlie gifts.

Thankfully, all the inventory was alphabetized. Walking along the rows, making my way past *H, I, J* and *K,* I reached *L* and scanned the item names stamped on the boxes. *Leapfrogs, Legos,* and *Lions, stuffed.* My eyes traveled upward. Laughing Lola just had to be atop this tall stack. Now I just needed to be ten feet tall. How?

Back by the elevator, I retrieved a librarian ladder on wheels and started pushing toward the *L* section. But it slid across the floor so easily that I climbed aboard and, with a big shove, was soon sailing between the rows. . . .

Woosh!

King of the warehouse, I imagined.

From my lofty position, I was able to see right over the wall of boxes a few rows over. Light brown boxes blurred as I glided, and then . . . a strange red flash of movement. Not again! Almost falling off the ladder, I quickly slid down and slammed my feet on the wheels, braking it handily in the *L* section.

"Hello?" I called out to the Red Phantom. "I know Kung Fu! Leave or I'll crush your spine!" I didn't know Kung Fu, but it sounded fierce . . . unless it was a real ghost. Maybe I should've threatened a spirit-sucking vacuum also.

Dead silence across the whole Inventory floor. Not a creature was stirring, not even a rat. I quickly scanned the room—all clear—and reached for the box of dolls. Lifting the cardboard box over my head, I heard a loud yap. Suddenly, I was face-to-face with bug eyes, a wet snout, and a pink tongue.

A mini-monster?!

Tumbling backward down the long ladder with my heart hammering, I sucked in a gasp. Arms flailing, I reached out desperately and barely caught hold of a rung to stop myself in midair. The box of Lolas wasn't so lucky—landing with a thump followed by sounds of eerie laughter as dozens of dollies giggled in unison. I shivered while catching my breath after the close call.

Daring to gaze upward, I realized I'd been half right about the rat. It was none other than Hercules, Kip's rat terrier. "Whew! How'd you get up here, tiny hiney?"

Hercules gave another loud yap, as if that explained anything. Climbing the ladder again, I coaxed him down and headed for the elevator with a dog in one arm and box of still chortling Lolas in the other. Noticing the pup's tiny stockings, I wondered if that was the flash of red I'd seen?

Maybe . . . maybe not.

Arriving underground on the RSS main floor—which I was still wrapping my head around—Kip was pacing anxiously, searching high and low. "He's right here," I called out, extending my hand with her prized pooch, his ears perking.

"Oh, Hercules! Thank you, Bub."

Kip looked right into my eyes, full of gratitude. Was it suddenly warm inside?

"Where was the little rascal?"

"Down, I mean up, in the Inventory section," I replied, my voice cracking. "By the way, is he a good climber? I found him on top of some, uh, toy boxes."

"I don't think so," Kip said, still nuzzling her baby. "Maybe if something scared him? It's been rumored a 'Red Phantom' stalks the warehouse . . . silly stuff. Maybe a mouse got in."

Before I could answer—

"Did you locate the stock, Bub?" Jett interrupted, tapping my ankle with his cane.

"Yeah, have it right here. Where do you need 'em?"

"C'mon. I'll teach you the shelf system," he said, strolling off— the blind leading the blind.

* * *

After our Choc-Nog break that afternoon, Kip and Hercules went up to Inventory; Austin and Jett worked on the mega-computer; and Wahoo wandered off to check the growing Christmas list. As usual, Mr. Mabrey sat in his glass-walled office, except now he slumped forward on his desk, head in his hands. The big boss looked tired . . . or maybe sad? It occurred to me that for the first time being here, no one was watching.

And the Crimson Crusher was awaiting her champion.

The mountain bike absolutely glowed after Austin's latest polish. Maybe I was torturing myself with a pipe dream. I hadn't even received my first paycheck; how would I ever make enough in time to bid on this prize?

Still, there was hope, and since I was a potential owner, it had to be fine to take her for a test-drive. At least no one had said otherwise, I rationalized . . . one of my foremost skills.

Hopping on, I swiveled my head in all directions to assure that I was alone. Then I pedaled slowly, steering in a nice, big circle in the middle of the warehouse. After building momentum, I glided and lifted my feet off the pedals to bask in the bliss of her smooth suspension and well-balanced tires.

Yap!

I screeched on the brakes. The front tire halted an inch from Hercules, almost indoor roadkill.

"Hercules! Hercules!" Kip's voice headed in my direction. Instantly, I jumped from the bike and set it back on its kickstand, whistling innocently. "Bub, you and Herc are becoming buds," Kip declared, spotting both of us. "Thanks, he needs lots of attention."

"What can I say? We're both fans of pretty girls in stockings," I replied with a wry smile as I scooped up the pooch and handed him over. Kip's cheeks turned scarlet, and she seemed to eye me with a newfound interest.

All in a day's work at RSS.

By shift's end that day, though, I had a headache and my thoughts were a jumble: cutie Kip, private Mr. Mabrey, financing my dream, the far-out warehouse, and creepy Red Phantom. I decided to walk off my muddled mind along Main Street. Maybe I'd check out Grant's Bike Boutique again to see if he had any more affordable models in stock—even a unicycle could be fun to test-drive.

Along the way, I passed Percy Pawn Shop, stopping to observe the array of sad and lonely things in the window display: someone's weathered cowboy hat, a diamond engagement ring, and a Junior Olympics silver medal forever valued by the winner. Most stores are about giving, but a pawn shop is about taking. They take your prized possession for a bargain price, then sell it to a stranger for profit if you can't afford to buy it back.

And most cannot, including my dad who'd been hoodwinked out of a Rolex watch years ago.

I heard someone humming and turned to see a young Latino boy about Chad's age, marching up Main Street with vigor. I couldn't take my eyes off his million dollar smile and skinny legs, clad in a pair of jet-black stockings.

He was too young to work at RSS, so surely his stockings were meant to keep his legs warm and weren't related to Wahoo's ranking system.

What did two black stockings mean anyway?

The boy's eyes met mine, and he grinned even wider than before. "Hi. Are you going inside?" he asked with a nod toward the pawn shop's entrance.

"Uh, nope, just window-shopping," I answered with a shrug.

The boy slid off one mitten and reached into his jacket pocket to remove an old coin. It was rusty and grimy, totally not what I was expecting. "Check this out," he said, flipping the small coin to me.

I smiled politely and turned it over in my hands, unable to

make out any printing. "Sorry, kid. I don't think you can buy squat with this."

With a laugh, the boy replied: "Hey, I don't want to spend it. I want to see how much it's worth."

"Oh," I said, giving the beat-up coin a second look.

"My grandpa gave it to me—just like his grandpa did to him when he was a boy. He said it might be worth something, and I wondered how much. But when I tried the other day, the Grinch running the pawn shop said return when I'm grown up. He wouldn't even check it. Can you go see what he'll offer you? I trust you."

I didn't hold out much hope for the kid, as the coin was in bad shape. But I knew how hurtful it can be when adults talk smack to kids. I nodded. "Sure, but don't expect a windfall. Okay?"

"What's a windfall?"

"A lot more than expected," I explained.

"I'll split it with you!" the boy said excitedly.

"Uh, I couldn't do that. It's yours," I shot back, knowing I could make some easy money, but it didn't feel right. "Look, how about I take it in and coax him to pay a few bucks, then you buy me a soda to cheer me up."

The boy looked sympathetic. "Cheer you up? Why?"

"Oh, nothing. I just want a new bike that I can't afford. Stupid me to reach for the stars."

"Don't worry, okay?" the boy said, patting me on the back. "If it helps get your bike, then keep the coin and whatever he pays for it."

I was amazed by his kindness, chalking it up to his age and trusting nature. How could he be offering up his grandfather's coin to a total stranger? What if he'd bumped into some hustler who'd take advantage? I'd pawn the coin and treat him fairly, despite his crazed sense of holiday goodwill. No Scrooge genes in this kid.

"Wait here . . . back in a jiffy. I'll bring you all I get for it," I swore.

The boy clapped his hands with glee! I winked and walked into the pawn shop, half-expecting grumpy Mr. Percy to laugh me right out of there.

Stepping casually toward the counter, I glanced with fake interest into the glass chests filled with gaudy displays of jewelry and timepieces. The entire time, I felt Mr. Percy's red-eyed glare peering over his thick-lens glasses. He was a corpulent, bald-headed man—not unlike a huge toad—with his neck and body squeezed into a green suit. I half-grinned as I imagined his slimy tongue lashing out and capturing the fly on the counter.

"Toy store's up the street, son," Mr. Percy croaked.

"I'm not shopping for toys, Mister," I said, putting on my game face. "I've got something you need to see. Hurry, I have important meetings."

I placed the coin on the counter. Despite my knees shaking, I stood like a soldier and puffed up my chest.

"I don't waste my time with—" Mr. Percy began to say, until he stopped and stared at the coin in front of him. "Is that . . . it is!" he asserted, whipping out a magnifying glass.

"You mean, it's got value?" I asked.

"A little rough around the edges, but it's always good to find a half-cent like this," he said, thrilled over polishing it.

A half-cent? That kid was going to be seriously disappointed.

"You've got a sharp eye, son, but times are tough. How much do ya want?"

"Five," I said, meaning five dollars.

"How 'bout four?"

"No, I'm sticking with five; take it or leave it." I'd seen my dad bargain like this before.

Frogman hesitated, rubbing the coin between his fingers, before answering: "Okay, okay, five hundred dollars . . . my absolute limit."

I almost lost it. Was he serious? I nodded quickly, stunned. Mr. Percy rambled on as he counted out fifty-dollar bills into my sweaty palm. He called the coin an "1805 Draped Bust half-cent" and said if uncirculated (clean and new), it would've been worth way more.

Holy Moly!

I stumbled out onto the icy street corner, but the boy wasn't standing outside. I checked up and down the street, around the corner, even stupidly under some nearby cars. And I couldn't call him or go after him; I didn't have a number or address or even a name. The mystery kid had left me all the goods—true to his promise. I just stood there with his $500, now seemingly mine, as not even the police could locate a random kid. I seriously could not believe my luck. The Crimson Crusher was at last within my grasp.

For the first time that holiday season, I felt overwhelmed with a sense of joy. The kind of joy one has when opening the perfect present. Even though I hadn't earned it, the cheery kid had made my entire Christmas season with his act of charity. And I didn't know if we'd ever cross paths again.

The next moment will always be frozen in time. Everything slowed to a crawl, but not because of the gift. It happened because I saw trouble brewing on the corner.

An impressive man in a suit was stepping from the curb with a cell phone to his ear . . . and a speeding car was hurtling straight at him!

CHAPTER 7

On instinct, I grabbed the man's arm, yanking him back. He glared in startled anger for a split second before the car, a flashy green blur, screeched by—missing him by inches!

Initially, the man acted like I was stealing his watch. And meanwhile, the driver of the green car seemed none the wiser, as I caught only the top of a curly head, bending over to grab something.

And then it was over. A splash of icy water washed up from the gutter and drenched our shoes. As the car sped off in a cloud of exhaust fumes, it must've dawned on the man that, by some miracle, I'd dragged him to safety. And I was just coming to terms with it all myself. Bub Olney—superhero and Stockling in Training—had saved the day!

Well, at least I was a Stockling candidate; superhero would have to wait.

"Th-thank you," the pale man stammered. "I was almost— you saved my life."

"No worries, glad you're okay," I muttered with a wave of my hand, trying to make light of it despite my shaky voice.

The man held up his cell phone that was yelling gibberish and disconnected without saying good-bye. "I should've paid better attention." The man gasped. "We just got in a ton of inventory that needs sorting, so I was distracted telling them where to put it. I'm the manager at Clarke's Department Store," the dazed man said before shaking my hand. "Let me introduce myself: Charles Dixon. And your name?"

"Bart, but call me Bub," I said, impressed. Clarke's was the biggest store in town, with five floors of upscale merchandise, including one dedicated to sports and toys.

"Well, Bub, I'm so pleased to meet you, since I'd be spending Christmas in a hospital—or worse—if I hadn't!" he declared, as some color returned to his cheeks. "Won't you let me show you my gratitude? Next time you visit the store, ask to see me. I'll treat you to a special gift. The least I can do." The gentleman handed me his card.

I didn't expect anything in return for the rescue, just had acted reflexively, but I was ecstatic over a bonus gift. After Mr. Dixon shook my hand to thank me again, he checked both ways before waving and departing.

Walking home with renewed energy, I considered my change of fortune. With my first RSS paycheck pending, plus the $500 windfall from the coin and gift for saving Mr. Dixon, I was a lot richer than when I'd left for work that day. If I played my cards right, I had a fighting chance to win the Christmas jackpot. With luck like mine, who needed a four-leaf clover?

Rounding the corner onto my street, I saw Chad shoveling the walk beside crotchety Mrs. Kirby's house. Moving closer, I realized the snow was several feet deep, probably collecting for days. No surprise, since the lady didn't leave her roost often except to chase away apple-snitchers during season. Her apples were always crisp and juicy, or so I'd been told.

Chad grunted as he dug in with the shovel, the metal scraping against concrete. "How's it going?" I asked. Despite the cold, his brow and scruffy mop of hair looked moist.

"All right," he answered flatly before digging back into the massive snow drift. He seemed to be still upset with me.

"Need a hand?" I asked.

"I dunno." Chad thought about it. "I only make three bucks for each sidewalk, so . . ."

There was no way I'd take money from my kid brother. Especially since I was richer than the Kitchen Kitty after my banner day.

"Well, if you're sure . . ." I teased and pretended to start for home. Chad shot me a death stare, so I didn't leave him hanging for long. "Just kidding, bro. Of course, I'll help, and you don't have to split the money with me. I'll grab another shovel."

Chad let out a sigh. "Thanks, I'm beat."

I jogged home and back with Dad's extra shovel, then got to work.

As we dug in, I kept sneaking glances at Chad. The kid had to labor twice as hard as me just to clear half as much space. "How many walks have you done today?" I asked, hoping it was more than this one.

"My fourth, and it's tough with so much ice," he said. It was like all his happiness had been depleted, and I couldn't deny the source. If I'd not rained on his Christmas parade, he'd be at home stringing popcorn and cranberries instead of this torture.

"Still saving up for the Beast?" I asked, trying to sound upbeat.

"I guess," Chad answered. "But no way I'll have enough by Christmas. What about your girly pink bike?"

"Uh . . . not sure . . . and it's red, not pink!" I didn't have the heart to tell him about the easy cash I'd been gifted; I had to do something to cheer him up. "Hey, looks like you missed a spot there, bro," I said mischievously as I flicked snow from my shovel onto his boots.

Chad's eyes lit up—still some life in him, after all. He flicked an even bigger pile directly onto my boots. "Be careful when you shovel, Bub," he said with a smirk.

"Oh, yeah?" I flung a huge scoop right at him, covering his front jacket in snow.

"This is war!" he shouted, giggling and dousing me with freezing flakes.

Before long, we had made a slushy, fun mess of the walk and laughed heartily before clearing it again and heading home. Still shoving each other along the way, we arrived at our front doorstep.

"What're you scoundrels up to?" Dad asked as he crutch-hobbled from his garage workshop toward the front door. He was wearing only a sweater and jeans, so we moved aside to let him enter the warm house first. "Thanks, but go ahead; you two are soaked head to toe," he said while holding open the front door.

"Hustle inside and clean up. Dinner soon." He chuckled before limping into the den.

We dashed up to our rooms to change, where I stashed the bills inside a Lego box under my bed. Perfect for overnight storage, and I'd carry it in my pocket during the day.

All angles covered.

I slid into my seat at the table and smirked at Chad while sniffing the steam rising from the crock-pot of stew. "Smells like victory," I teased, referring to our snow battle.

"Puh-lease," he scoffed, crossing his arms while Mom placed a ladle into the crock-pot.

"Well, go on, help yourself," she said to me, closest to the pot.

My parents took seats opposite each other. They seemed to be licking their lips, but both plates were bare—probably waiting until Chad and I had served ourselves. When it was their turn to dive in, they scooped only half-portions. *Must not be hungry*, I figured. Yet, I could've sworn that Mom's stomach growled when we rested forks on our plates. And later I would see Dad munching crackers in the kitchen after putting dirty dishes in the sink to soak.

Before we'd escaped the table, Mom's eyes darted from Chad to me. "Why don't we do something tonight as a family. Game night?"

Ugh. "Game night's kind of cheesy, Mom," I replied.

"What do you mean?" she said, offended. "You guys used to stay up all night playing holiday games. Remember *Rudolph's Rainbow*?"

I glanced at Chad . . . his heart wasn't in it either, unlike past years. "That crazy reindeer game bit the dust—his deformed red nose never lit up. How 'bout charades?" I said, trying to atone.

"Exactly!" Mom agreed, grinning. "Great idea, Bub."

I groaned inwardly but smiled as we all assembled around the crackling fire. Dad volunteered to go first while the rest of us hatched ideas. Most of his attempts were riffs on limping heroes in books, TV, and film: *Treasure Island*/Long John Silver, *Moby Dick*/Captain Ahab, and Hopalong Cassidy, who'd starred in classic cowboy films before my day. Mom guessed Hopalong easily, earning catcalls from Chad and me.

As I sat trying to think of a charade that avoided prancing around like a one-legged clown in a sack race, the only image I visualized was the kid with the old coin.

And I didn't even know his name.

"You're up, Bub," Mom said with a wink. She was enjoying hanging with her boys, even if it was just a lame game of charades. Checking her watch, she added: "Half an hour before I leave, so let's make it snappy, pappy." Dad smiled at her cuteness.

"Okay," I said, donning my game face and trying to be creative, before it hit me. "Got one. It's a saying."

First, I flicked an imaginary coin in the air, and after guessing things like "coin" and "money" they all settled on the word "penny." Then I pretended to offer the penny to my family before pointing to my head a few times, until Dad guessed, "Penny for your thoughts!" When I gave the thumbs-up, he winked and raised a crutch to tap his own head.

Even Chad looked amused.

I breathed a sigh of relief that my turn was over. Now it was time for Mom to go to work, breaking up our little party. She whipped around the room, pecking us on the cheek, before waving as she headed out the door. "Gotta run. Fun game, like olden days, love ya!" she said.

Yet I was too far away to wave properly—the lucky penny still on my mind. Flipping in the air, turning over and over as I stared deeply into red embers of the fire. It was soon joined by an imaginary cascade of shiny silver dollars, pouring into my hands until overflowing. Five hundred dollars raining from the sky . . . a flurry of riches!

But somehow—as Mom left to work the midnight shift again, and Dad teetered back out to his garage, and Chad counted and recounted his hard-earned bucks—my good fortune felt like a sneaky secret. The Kitchen Kitty was even sicker, now reduced to $200, and I was . . . well, very lucky. My crimson dream with summer of freedom was miraculously in sight. So why did I feel like retching?

Food poisoning? Hormones? A virus?

I shook it off before climbing into bed. Still, all night I tossed and turned like a Laughing Lola in a hurricane. Tomorrow I would discuss my strategy with Wahoo to bid on the insurmountable Crimson Crusher.

And finally discover if my newfound fortune guaranteed a very Merry Christmas—at least for one Bartholomew Murrah Olney.

CHAPTER 8

"Take it," I said, laying the crisp notes on Wahoo's desk in a stack. I'd counted the bills half a dozen times that morning before arranging them into a block of cash, like paying off a ransom. And this ransom would free the captive bike of the century.

"What's this?" Wahoo asked, raising an eyebrow.

It was my first time inside her office. Behind her was a bookcase crowded with gleaming trophies. On the walls, photographs of Wahoo grinned back at me, all dawn or dusk scenes, each with a different backdrop. There was a panorama of the African savannah encircling her in one shot; Wahoo alongside a beautiful Norwegian fjord in another; and an underwater pic with both thumbs-up beside a magnificent coral reef. Her world outside work had been chock-full of adventure, but in the meantime. . . .

My focus returned to RSS Wahoo—sitting at a small desk— her hands resting beside two phones, one pad, a pink feather quill, and an inkpot. She was blinking at me, waiting calmly for my response. "Uh . . . it's my downposit."

"Your whatsit?"

"My downposit . . . you know, the down payment, deposit, for the bike. Five hundred dollars. And I was hoping that, along with my first week's paycheck, you'd call it a done deal and take the bike off the market."

I smiled the smile that always coaxed Mom to say yes.

Wahoo wrinkled her nose—not a good sign. I had witnessed her many faces, but this was the closest to a scowl. "I won't be played like a violin. It's not for sale, Bub. You know that."

"Sale . . . auction . . . same difference. Will you take my money? Please?"

"Sorry, it's against RSS policy. I could be deflamitigated, which isn't pretty." And with that, she resumed staring at the pad on her desk that was blank—like my brain at the moment.

My shoulders slumped. No dice. With a frown, I scooped up the cash and shoved it back into my pocket. "RSS policy" seemed like a phony excuse to say no without explaining.

Suddenly, one of the two phones on her desk rang, flashing red and green and moving like it was alive. I noticed a pair of metallic springs had sprung from the bottom of the phone, making it impossible to ignore.

Wahoo grabbed the receiver and held it to her ear. "Certainly, Mr. Mabrey, I'll proceed," she answered. This had to be an internal phone—direct to her boss's office.

She stared at me, then hung up. Suspecting it was time to leave, I walked to the door with a Wahoo-shaped shadow trailing behind. She was hot on my heels. "Uh, going my way?" I asked, feeling awkward.

"I have an announcement for you and the Stocklings," she said, almost running me over. Once back into the warehouse fray,

Wahoo whistled loudly and shouted: "All wise Stocklings, gather 'round . . . something confidential!"

Who could resist that teaser?

The Coreys, Hivers, and Fixers all bumbled forward into a wonky sort of lineup—a row of stocking-clad Stocklings and one jean-clad newbie. Wahoo stood before us, waiting patiently with a blank pad in her outstretched hand. With flair, she raised a pink, feather quill and scratched something on the page. The only hitch: From my view, I could see that absolutely nothing was being written. The page remained as blank as a snowy field. But she admired her writing with a smile, licking the tip of her quill and finalizing her note with a confident dot—an invisible period, no doubt.

What planet was she from?

Catching my eye, Kip nodded. "Invisible ink," she whispered. "Wahoo loves toys like the rest of us. She got a well of invisible ink in her stocking when young and still writes memos with it. Cool, huh?"

"But how does she know what she wrote if she can't see it?" I asked, distracted by Kip standing close to me and her gardenia scent.

"Well, she remembers it, silly," Kip tittered. "The memos are to herself. And when you think about it, the act of writing it down is a key part of memorizing." I half-nodded, listening to Kip's explanation, sorry I'd asked a sensible question about the nonsensical. "And Wahoo enjoys picking the right words," Kip continued. "Look how pleased she is with whatever she corrected."

I looked over and had to agree. Humming absently, she appeared as happy as a bug in a rug while staring at the unseen words on her pad. Wahoo's world . . . sweet, if quirky.

"Okay, pipe down," she ordered, hushing the Coreys and Fixers as they bickered over repairing one shelving unit to stop the clockwise rotation of the handle from spilling stock.

I remained silent during the RSS family feud.

"Well, make sure you do fix it; that's your job, Fixers!" Jett concluded the argument.

"We have a special event ahead of us," Wahoo began, consulting her blank note pad again. "Mr. Mabrey has requested all hands on deck to stay overnight tomorrow at RSS, to assist with a mystery and whatever." During a smattering of whispers, everyone seemed to be eyeing me up and down. "And you'll be paid overtime, of course," Wahoo assured, as if she'd read my mind. Maybe she saw not only invisible words, but invisible thoughts too. I just hoped that she didn't see ghosts.

As we disbanded, my mind reeled with the idea of earning extra money. Maybe I could raise the stakes with Wahoo to accept my offer, or worst-case scenario, I'd have a fatter wallet to win the auction. Also, my curiosity was piqued by the intrigue of this special event. "So, we'll sleep here?" I nudged Austin.

"If you're lucky. You'll prob'ly be too hyped. There'll be lots to do, but, yeah, we might catch some shuteye if you survive Jett's snoring like a warthog." Austin chuckled.

"I heard that!" yelled Jett as he got ready to crank the shelves around. "I snore because you bore." They snickered in unison.

Sleep or not, did I really want to stay in this creepy warehouse at night? It was weird enough during the day. I winked at Austin and returned to work. Whatever "whatever" was, it sounded like an adventure was in store for me too.

* * *

After getting my parents' approval for the sleepover—not an easy task—I felt butterflies of excitement for the rest of the night. When morning arrived, I tucked my toothbrush and clothing into an overnight bag, headed for RSS and walked (well, squeezed) through the small door into the warehouse.

Immediately, it seemed that all Stocklings had me in their sights. What on Earth had I done to deserve this?

Would this be like my first experience with the Drink-o-na-tor—only much worse than having chocolate milk in my ears? Would the walls of the warehouse close in on me once and for all? Or would I finally meet the Red Phantom—in a dangerous game of hide-and-seek?

Before my mind raced too far ahead, I decided to rein it in and have as normal a day as possible at the abnormal RSS, Inc. I beamed a silly grin, although Kip kept sizing me up—legs in particular. And Wahoo was stealing glances, before consulting her empty pad to make quick, invisible notes.

I ran my socks off all day, filling orders as fast as they spooled out of Austin's printer, then delivering them to Jett's shelves. In the windowless confines of the warehouse, I had no idea how late it was until my sixth trip up to the Inventory floor. The partially blocked windows were now a menacing shade of black. Night had fallen.

Flicking on a switch, I shed some light on the situation. Boxes upon boxes were stacked to such heights that left little room for ceiling lamps to shine down. Now it was apparent that these weren't ordinary lamps—more of Mr. Mabrey's mechanical ingenuity. The entire ceiling was outfitted with a mosaic of tiny mirrors, and the switch I'd flicked had cleverly unplugged a hole in the roof. The light above me was a reflection of the moon in the sky outside the building.

Full moon for werewolves, I thought with a chill.

Mr. Mabrey was a smart fellow, using natural light sources to save money, hand cranks to turn the hulking shelves, even steam power to run the Drink-o-nator. He probably used every penny saved on electricity to procure the wealth of toys. I wouldn't have put it past him to run Austin's computer using puppy power from Hercules on a miniature treadmill.

At last, I headed back to the main floor for my final assignment of the night.

"One more item, for Nicole in LA, then it's party time," Austin said, pointing to the printer whirring out a sheet of paper. His comment hinted at the evening's events.

"Got it," I said, snatching up the paper and heading for the elevator, almost pressing Down before hitting the Up button. The elevator doors promptly slid open, and I stepped inside. Curiously, a strange patch of water on the floor resembled two wet footprints. Had someone recently walked in here, wearing snow-covered boots? The ride up was unusually bumpy.

Stepping out, I noticed more fresh, wet prints leading off into the shadows of the Inventory area. It was puzzling since, to my knowledge, nobody but me had worked there during the day. But what did I know? So, I shrugged and warily went to work, seeking one box of Super Stompers—kiddie boots that stomped monster-shaped holes in mud or ice. Thankfully, this time they were on a lower shelf than Laughing Lolas, easily reachable without a ladder.

Creak!

I spun around, my heart racing. That was a strange noise, no doubt about it. While I don't always trust my eyes, my ears had detected something loud and, even worse, very close by. I searched all around me—left, right, down, up . . . up again!

Above me, a ceiling fan was loudly creaking and gyrating wildly, as if a bolt had loosened. Just then, the bolt completely gave way, dropping the fan's lethal blades down . . . down to where I was standing—dumbstruck!

Instantly, a *red blur* zoomed into view and pushed me. I felt two gloved hands, strong yet gentle, shoving my body backward. And then, more red—a sea of red whipping past my face as I tumbled into a giant, soft bag of Bouncy Balls, right before hearing a resounding crash!

In a daze, I looked up and over to where I'd just stood. In my place was the ceiling fan, lying with its blades in pieces, over a jagged crack in the floor. While the red figure was nowhere to be seen, there were several puddled footprints left behind, the only hard evidence of another living person on this floor.

As I backed up, a stiff hand from behind nudged my shoulder! Electrified, I spun around and found myself facing a giant *Nutcracker Soldier* on its side, with one foot broken off. His wooden smile and spectral eyes looked haunting. Almost slipping in a puddle, huffing and puffing, I sprinted to the elevator and pressed the Down button furiously. "Help!" I cried out, hoping someone was in range. No response—I was ready to hide, but I pressed the button once more.

Gently.

It worked.

After finding Wahoo below and blurting out my story about facing death and a Red Phantom who'd rescued me, she calmed me down and asked for details. Still breathless, I invited her up to the Inventory level to investigate.

However, the wet footprints had somehow vanished into thin air.

As invisible as Wahoo's ink.

CHAPTER 9

Wahoo guessed that I'd been dazed and confused by the falling Nutcracker toy that had miraculously pushed me from harm's way. I was known for my vivid imagination, but this seemed real. She declared: "Trust me, Bub, you're still discombobulated from the fall. A Fixer search found nothing nefarious on the premises—no Red Phantom, no real Bandersnitch. I can assure you every living person is accounted for."

Living person? Reassuring . . . not! She wasn't a horror film guru like me, but I just nodded and didn't mention undead zombies can still eat your liver. Indeed, all humans were accounted for, as I realized when the elevator delivered us to the assembly on the main floor.

Every single Stockling was standing and grinning, waiting for someone or something to arrive. Still a bit wobbly, I scanned the crowd for a surprise guest and asked Wahoo: "What's going on? Who are they waiting for?"

There was no one except. . . .

"You. They're waiting for you."

"Why?" I said, mystified. "I thought we were preparing for a special event?" The entire group seemed ready to applaud, but for what I had no clue.

"Indeed," Wahoo replied, her arm around me, guiding me from the elevator into the center of the warehouse. "The special event is your initiation into the Red Stocking Society! You're about to earn your stockings, Bub. What you do with them remains to be seen."

That's when I noticed the Coreys, Hivers, and Fixers stepping aside to reveal a table, upon which rested two black stockings. All the hullabaloo suggested I was about to be knighted with a pair of floppy, long socks. Sir Lancelot, eat your heart out.

"All this trouble . . . for me?" I asked anxiously, realizing I was in the spotlight. My recent encounter with the Red Phantom didn't help either.

"Like I've said before, Bub, you're special. You've got some issues, join the crowd, but your core is good, so now we invite you into our family if you qualify." Resolute, Wahoo pointed to the stockings, and somehow I knew my life was changed *forever*.

Hesitantly, I picked them up. Very soft. Kip smiled and mouthed the words, "I knitted for you." Blushing, I averted my gaze to examine the goods. The black stockings were reversible— bright red on the inside—maybe for use at another ceremony with trumpets and unicorns? Actually, unicorns were boring compared to flying reindeer with oddball names like Donner and Blitzen. Was my head still reeling?

As I bent down to remove my own socks, Wahoo frowned like I was breaking an unwritten rule. "Not so fast. First you must take the oath of mission and secrecy."

Whoa! This I hadn't bargained for. After the stocking gift, now I had to make some big vow?

Wahoo unrolled a large scroll across the table. Plain as day, recorded in longhand with black ink, there it was:

The STOCKLING Credo
To attain rank of RSS Stockling and promote the Christmas spirit of giving and good cheer, I promise to be, to the best of my ability:
>*Responsible*
>*Diligent*
>*Sensitive*
>*Truthful*
>*Compassionate*
>*Kind*
>*Nurturing*
>*Generous.*

Also, I will strive to keep Santa wonder alive and perform at least one golden deed during each Christmas season. Furthermore, I promise to keep all of this secret within the Society.

It caught my eye that the first letter of each word cleverly spelled RD STCKNG—an abbreviation for ReD SToCKiNG. Then I noticed the last paragraph. What the heck was Santa wonder? Like not crushing your little brother's belief in Santa? I'd already learned my lesson on that one.

"Where do I sign?" I asked, as many Stocklings laughed into their hands.

Wahoo pointed to the scroll. "You don't sign this, Bub. You pledge it—then live up to it."

My eyes danced from the crowd to the script and back again. Kip smiled warmly at me; Austin gave me a goofy thumbs-up; and the impish twinkle was back in Wahoo's eyes. I wasn't sure what a "golden deed" was, but I knew that I was beginning to trust the Stocklings as my friends. And I certainly didn't want to quash anyone else's Christmas spirit—even though Santa Claus was bogus in my opinion. I recited the credo in my clearest voice.

Once I was done reading aloud, I smiled and held up the stockings for all to see. The animated crowd seemed ready to clap, but nobody did. Even when I rolled up my jeans and put them on—both warm as toast—nothing happened. Was there more to the ceremony? A Christmas carol sing-along? A cookie-decorating contest? A broken ornament swap?

"Here you go," said Wahoo, handing me three envelopes stamped with the red RSS logo.

"Should I open them?" I asked, unsure of the next step in this rousing ritual.

"Later," Wahoo advised. "These are letters to Santa, hand-selected by Mr. Mabrey just for you, Bub."

Surveying the room, I spied Mr. Mabrey standing behind his desk in the glass-walled office, except this time he was playing the saxophone. I found it strange that the one person I hadn't officially met, the only one missing from the RSS team, was the head honcho himself. He was even more intriguing than Wahoo. Mr. Mabrey must have known who I was and had even hand-picked letters for me—yet he hadn't bothered to attend my important event?

Maybe he was only rolled out for super special occasions . . . like an elf retirement party.

"I know the computer sorts all of the letters automatically," I said, shocked that I'd be reading someone's private Santa mail. "And then prints a list of orders to fulfill. Do you want me to haul these gifts from upstairs, as usual?"

"Not quite," Wahoo replied. "Instead of using Inventory items, these wishes will require more from you. This could be your red-letter day, but you'll have to call on your wits plus a certain thumping organ to succeed. Remember?" She gently patted my chest.

Her clever words blew past me as I focused only on "require more from you." I glanced at the Stocklings, fearful I was about to bite off more than I could chew. I loved horror films, action thrillers, and holiday dramas, but I never planned on starring in one. I was just a mixed up kid. "Okay, give me the low-down on the showdown," I quipped.

Wahoo turned serious. "Here's the drill: Three letters, three wishes. By high noon tomorrow, you must fulfill these wishes with good deeds—at least one *golden*."

"Golden deed?"

"Golden deeds are pure and selfless. And you just swore to complete one golden deed each holiday season."

I did? Oh, yes, I did. What had I gotten myself into? "Okay, sounds cool, but how can I tell a regular good deed from a golden one?"

"It's something you'll feel . . . all I can say."

Clear as mud—as usual. "Okay, so how do I get started?"

"Well, it's too late for online shopping and shipping, but since stores stay open late for Christmas, you have a couple of hours tonight. Stay on Main Street or well-lit surrounding areas, and RSS will ensure your safety."

"Thanks, I think. Sounds like this could interrupt my sleep; I might get cranky." I tried to keep the skeptic out of my voice.

"Never said it would be a piece of cake. Your task is difficult; we expect you to be tough. Just like your dad who was a stellar Marine."

How did she know that? "And if I fail?"

"Then you're off the payroll, and your time here is done. Back to the simple life."

I tried to keep my mouth from flopping open like a bass. Seriously? If I couldn't complete this crazy game, I was out of a job? Even worse, I knew that I'd lose my chance to win the bicycle lottery and continue gorging on the most delicious drinks ever.

I stared at Kip again, and she offered a sympathetic smile. "*R-E-D*," she mouthed. Red? As in red stockings?

"Wait, is this why some Stocklings have red and others have black stockings?" I asked.

"Now you're thinking before blinking!" Wahoo said. "If you achieve all of these deeds by noon, you can reverse one stocking to red, earning S3 status in the Red Stocking Society."

"What's an S3? Sounds like army rank." I hoped it meant a pay raise or privileges that might help rescue my bike from the evil auctioneer.

Wahoo inhaled deeply before commanding: "Bring out the big board for bodacious Bub!"

Was this the part of the ceremony where I'd be tortured?

The crowd parted again, and one of the Fixers wheeled in a massive, rolling white board and parked it right next to Wahoo. "Welcome to the S-Game, Bub . . . a game like no other!"

The board featured an illustration of a huge Christmas tree with a red ladder leaning against it. Along the ladder, from top to bottom:

The S-Game: SANTA BOARD RANKING*

Truth and wisdom will abound, as the cycle goes around . . .

S1—Top of the Ladder: Real Deal Santa Claus!

S2—Stocklings Who Create Santa Magic for Individuals or Groups (Two Red Stockings)

S3—Stocklings Who Perform Golden Deeds Each Season (One Black, One Red Stocking)

S4—Santa Portrayers in Stores, Parades, Performing Arts

S5—Santa Believer Alumni Who Keep the Magic Alive

S6—Kid Santa Believers

*Only S3 Stocklings are eligible for S2 rank. Non-Stocklings with S5 and S4 rank unable to serve at an RSS, Inc. facility may attain Honorary S3 or S2 rank by achieving goals. Always be Santastic!

I stared at the board for awhile, then eyeballed the other Stocklings and their combinations of red and black stockings. My plain jeans suddenly felt conspicuous. I wasn't even a lowly S6 or S5—at least not since I'd ruined Chad's belief in Santa magic. "What does 'cycle goes around' mean? Anything to do with that sign above the front door?" I asked Wahoo.

She nodded knowingly. "Yep, the sign reminds us life is a cycle. Someday you'll understand."

"Okay . . . so are you an S1?"

My Stockling muse chuckled. "Don't be vacuous, Bub. Santa is the one and only S1."

Of course . . . Santa . . . the esteemed Mr. Claus, North Pole version, back into the equation.

Refraining from rolling my eyes, I nodded while scanning the crowd of expectant Stocklings again. Then in one last try to bring down the house with applause, I held the letters up high. Still nothing. I felt disrespected and decided to leave; maybe this secret society jazz wasn't for me. I had two chances of moving up the ladder: slim and none. Impetuously, I started walking away.

Just then, Wahoo whispered into my ear: "Time to put up or shut up. Your call." I stopped in my tracks. Her bold challenge turned me back around.

Without another word, the Stocklings disbanded. Nobody clapped or waved; they all just ambled off in different directions, returning to work, including Wahoo, who holed up in her office. In seconds there was no one in sight, and the Santa Board loomed ominously over me. I was left with three random letters, wearing two black stockings, with one mission to deliver Christmas gifts for three lucky kids before twelve noon. Too much math for one day. I just hoped none of them requested a Schwinn Crimson Crusher.

Opening the first envelope, I pulled out a letter. Squinting, I strained to decipher the kid's handwriting in the dim light of the warehouse: "Dear Santa, I want a nice puppy for Christmas."

Some kids dream of bikes or video games or footballs, but this one—a ten-year-old named Howie—wanted a living, breathing creature for Christmas. Maybe Kip would consider donating her pup Hercules for a good cause? I knew the answer: She would boot me out the door quicker than Wahoo. I chuckled before getting serious. Since all of my money was reserved for the Crusher fund, where could I locate a free canine fast? I doubted the pound would let me adopt a dog without parents in tow.

Lots of ideas paraded through my head . . . until a light bulb clicked on. I knew exactly where to find a free dog—literally, running free. Bugsy!

I reminded myself that the nightmare about him wasn't real.

I'd just have to lure Bugsy into RSS, knock him senseless, spray insecticide, and my first good—maybe golden—deed was in the bank. Oh, I almost forgot his rabies shot. Hopefully Howie wouldn't mind a grumpy pooch with attitude . . . not exactly nice.

Then I remembered Bugsy's saliva-covered fangs and him snapping at my heels as he chased me through the woods, munching on my back jean pocket. How would I ever put a bow on that monster?

On second thought. . . .

Kip joined me with a plate of chocolate chip cookies and Hercules barking in my ear. "Got any ideas yet, Bub? Time's ticking away," she said with concern on her face.

"Um, yeah." It was settled. I wouldn't cut corners by using Hercules or Bugsy to solve my dilemma. Needing to hit the pavement, I thanked Kip for the cookie feast, even told her a joke. Holding a cookie in each hand, I cracked: "I eat a balanced diet—chocolate in both hands!" As she giggled, I grabbed my coat and boots and hotfooted off.

I wasn't sure how to do it, but I didn't want to let down my new friends . . . or lose out on my paychecks and any hope of bidding on the bike. The good news: My Crimson Crusher was still within reach. The bad news: Checking the time and knowing that I hadn't even begun, my golden quest seemed impossible.

CHAPTER 10

I hurried outside, only to be slapped in the face by the night's frosty air. If not in alert mode before, that did the trick. Less than fifteen hours until high noon tomorrow and three deeds to fulfill; no time for lollygagging, as Mom would say. I had to make these hours count before all stores on Main Street flipped their signs to "Closed."

Luckily, I only needed one to be open—the pet store.

Approaching the dimly lit street that twinkled with Christmas lights and festive displays, I caught sight of a shadow trailing behind. Like a spy film, I first checked for traffic, crossed to the other side of Main, then jogged back again. Yes, someone still on my tail. Wahoo had promised dependable RSS would ensure my safety, but I didn't expect a personal bodyguard.

Likely a Fixer, hopefully not a wimp.

Just don't slow me down, I thought.

I glanced backward. About twenty feet to the rear, my protector was dressed head-to-toe in black, like a ninja, with a knit cap resting above sunglasses. Yes, he was wearing shades at night and moved with catlike stealth . . . treading lightly, avoiding the crunchy snow and crushed ice. The only hint that he was alive was the fog exhaling from his mouth—or maybe steam?

I tried to focus on the task at hand, mapping out Main Street in my mind. The pet store was at the far end, about a mile, so I needed to hustle. Even with extended holiday shopping hours, it was going to be tight. But first things first: I was parched from scarfing down cookies without milk, so the convenience store farther down Main awaited like a desert oasis. A lightning-fast pit stop was in order.

I turned around to tell my tracker where we'd be going, but he'd vanished. Or slipped into a dark corner, or become invisible? Maybe he needed a pit stop too.

Either way, I was alone.

Halfway down Main, I reached the convenience store and suddenly recalled the bulging wad of cash in my pocket. The $500 had totally slipped my mind; I was a pickpocket's delight. Or worse?

I shook off my nerves and hung a right into Main Street Mini-Mall. In my other pocket was the fiver from Dad, so thankfully I wouldn't need to break a fifty in public. A bottle of yellow pineapple juice seemed fitting for a golden quest, so I snatched one from the cooler and started sipping it on my way back to the familiar cashier.

Marching forward, I could see Mr. Phillips standing beside the cash register, his eyes as shrouded in bags as the groceries he'd just sold to a senior. The store owner's tired expression reminded me of the late hour; I needed to keep moving. But in my hurry to grab the fiver, I picked my own pocket—the wrong one of course—and accidentally dropped the wad of cash in plain view.

My heart raced as I scrambled to pick up the fifty-dollar bills strewn on the floor. Pulling all the notes into a heap, I quickly stood and started shoving them into my pockets. And that's when I spotted him by the cooler—not my bodyguard, but a brawny teen wearing a red hockey jersey. His devilish eyes flanked a throbbing vein on his forehead. With one of his club-like hands, he rubbed the back of his thick neck, then grinned.

Not at me, but at my greenbacks.

Placing my drink on the counter and scarcely taking my eyes off the big dude, I slid the fiver over to Mr. Phillips. "Thanks, Bub. Be careful," he said, ringing it up.

"Keep the change," I mumbled, hurriedly, leaving an insane tip for a two dollar drink—my first tip ever. Meanwhile, Mr. Phillips shot his eyes toward the door, the message clear.

I gulped down most of the juice and tossed the bottle into a recycling bin with one last glance over my shoulder. The red-shirted rogue was paying Mr. Phillips, all the while watching me sideways. After a fruity burp of relief, I rushed back into the cold with a renewed sense of urgency.

Careful not to slip on ice coating the sidewalk, I jogged past the last ten shops to reach Pet Project. Thankfully, the lights were still on, although a gray-haired woman was sweeping the floor. I needed to think and act fast.

The $500 was burning a hole in my pocket, but that cash was earmarked for the Crimson Crusher freedom fund. Besides, I couldn't imagine that Wahoo expected Stocklings to buy these gifts with our own money . . . or would she? That didn't seem right, so I shook off the thought. Maybe I could just use my wits to fulfill all three golden deeds without depleting my own gold in the process.

"What to do, what to do?" I murmured. How could I finagle a free dog for this poor kid? Hmm . . . poor. Of course, that was it! I needed to look poor as a pauper.

Not homeless, but too-broke-to-buy-a-dog-for-Christmas poor, so the lady would feel sorry for me and donate a puppy to the cause. But how could I pull it off?

Another brainwave: Ducking behind a nearby trash receptacle on wheels, I slipped off my jacket and stowed it out of sight. A really poor kid wouldn't own a fleece-lined jacket like mine. Next, I peered into the bin, which was gross to the max: rotten green peppers mixed with cheese, charcoal with ash, piles of dust, dog food leftovers. Cringing, I scooped up some charcoal and dust and rubbed the debris all over my sweater. Then I grabbed a clump of bell pepper and cheese and smeared a green swath on both cheeks. The smell was enough to make Right Guard turn left, but I was sure nobody would mistake me for a kid with a fortune.

Returning to the pet store's window, I caught sight of my reflection in the glass. Ugh—I'd nailed it, resembling a scruffy urchin. If anyone at school ever saw me in this getup, good luck with the dating game. Then I noticed the happiest, scrappiest pup trying to catch my attention—panting tongue and wagging tail, paws against the window. He had a cool patch of brown over his left eye, the rest of him white as snow. I already knew his name.

The store worker, a bespectacled older lady, smiled and stopped sweeping. Balancing against her broom like a friendly witch, she gestured for me to enter.

A welcoming bell jingled as I hobbled inside with a fake limp, shivering. The store was warm and bright, reminding me how much I'd missed my jacket while freezing outside. The lady fixed her sights on me as her mouth curved into an *Oh*. I imagined her thoughts: Oscar the Grouch had come to life. But if she felt it, she surely didn't show it.

"Dearie, are you all right?" she asked with a kind voice. Sniffing the air, she backed up a bit.

"I'm fine, ma'am," I answered politely. "Just admiring your pups. They look mighty friendly, and I could really use a buddy right now."

Had I overplayed it?

Her wrinkled face relaxed. "Go say hello. Pet them if you like. I'm just cleaning up shop for the night. I'm Barbara, the owner."

"Thank you, ma'am, feels good to be in a warm place," I said, rubbing my arms with another shiver that was real.

"Can I get you something? A cup of tea, maybe? I have a kettle out back," she said before adding: "You'll catch your death in this weather."

"Oh, I'm good. You get used to numbness after a while."

Murmuring to herself, Barbara continued to sweep up cat and dog hair.

I wandered over to the box of puppies next to the store window and reached down to Patch, patting him gently on the head. He yapped cheerily at me, and I grinned back. Even cuter than Hercules, though I'd never tell Kip. Howie would adore this pooch. Who wouldn't?

I glanced at Barbara and weakly smiled. "Is everything okay, dear?" she asked with concern, touching my arm.

"Yes. It's just that . . . I think this one really likes me."

"He has his shots; would you care to take him home with you? You do have shelter?" she quizzed, her drawn-on eyebrows arching higher.

"Yes, my new friend and I should be out of the elements if we sleep in the garage. Especially when they fix the roof to keep rodents out. Thanks for caring."

"Oh, good," Barbara sighed with relief. "Well, he seems to have taken to you too. These pups are a mixed breed. I usually charge fifty dollars, but I could make you a deal for . . . half price."

By now I'd picked up Patch, who was licking the side of my face, trying to taste the nasty green goo on my cheek. This dog had an iron stomach.

"Just one detail, ma'am," I added, building to the big finish. "I don't have any money."

"Oh," she replied softly, breaking the record for saying "Oh" so many times in a day.

I just waited, blinking at her and letting Patch blink in unison. We were quite the team. Impossible to resist. . . .

Finally, she caved.

"Oh, go on then. As long as you both stay warm—promise me."

"Promise!" I exclaimed on my way to the door, Patch in my arms. "Thank you very much. Howie will—I mean, *I* am so happy!"

"Wait. Take this." Barbara removed a shawl from her shoulders and bundled it around Patch and me. "It's chilly out there. Merry Christmas, you two," she said, her eyes teary.

I was touched that she would give away a dog plus donate clothing off her back to keep us toasty. My pauper impression had worked better than expected. No doubt, this lady was charged with Christmas spirit.

During my hasty exit, she even threw in a couple of Snickers bars. How could I top this?

"Merry Christmas!" I shouted back. The bell jingled as I waved good-bye, holding Patch. Outside it was snowing heavily now. I grabbed my hidden jacket and slipped into it over the shawl, zipping it so that both of our heads poked from the neckline.

Off we went, the two-headed dog-boy creature, on our way back to RSS. I was checking off my first deed, and it wasn't even bedtime. There might even be time to celebrate with airborne chocolate milk from the Drink-o-nator.

As I trudged onward, most of the lights on Main Street flickered off. Closing time. A bitter wind blasted me, and Patch snuggled even closer. Did I hear a tapping sound coming up from behind? I whirled around to see an old man, meandering with his cane and carrying a wrapped present in his other hand.

Innocent enough, but I was on edge.

"Happy Holidays!" the man greeted as he turned south to cross an eerily empty street.

"Cheers!" I shouted, then walked past Toby's Toys, where a colorful magic set on display caught my attention. I nuzzled Patch on his head while staring through the window.

Suddenly: "No more cheers, kid. Give me the money or you'll get clobbered!" ordered a coarse voice from behind. My chest tightened.

I spun around as Patch yapped a threatening bark. At first, all I saw was another red blur, moving fast in my direction. Instantly, the hockey-shirted teenager, looming larger than life, reached to grab my coat by the arm! My heart pounded as he yanked me toward him. I fought hard, desperate, bashing him with my free fist, but his burly hand held me in an iron grip.

"No! Help!" I cried out, foolish since I was all alone on a dark street.

But I wasn't alone.

Something caught my vision . . . from nowhere, a black streak turned into slashing arms and legs, moving swiftly as one unit. Chopping, swiping, kicking—a human tornado of energy and action! The bully hardly knew the score until he slammed to the ground, shattering an icy puddle, then moaning.

I tried but couldn't feel sorry for him. Turning to my rescuer, I stuttered, "Th-thank you—I . . . I . . ."

"No problem, Bub."

He knew me? The man removed his cap to reveal a shock of pink hair.

Then the sunglasses.

Wahoo stared back at me, grinning while catching her breath. "Forgot to mention, I'm head of Security too."

"What!" I exclaimed, shocked to the core.

"I just look like a wimp." She winked. "Those are martial arts trophies in my office. I'm a Taekwondo Black Belt but only fought since you were in danger." Then, seeing that I was still shaken, she remained silent, just holding my arm and supporting me.

Wahoo never ceased to be amazing!

Quivering, Patch buried himself inside my jacket.

"Thanks, he was going to rob and hurt me," I managed to say, trembling more than Patch.

Wahoo nodded and patted my shoulder, her presence a calming force. We stood there a moment as I collected my nerves. The thug tried standing until Wahoo forcefully constrained him. "Behave!" she ordered. Finally, he conceded and lay still.

"You should be more careful about who sees your money," she advised, her tone gentle, unlike her usual off-the-wall chatter at the warehouse.

I nodded back.

We started the trek back to RSS. When we were almost there, she turned to me, pinching her nose. "Bub, it's important to rest up for tomorrow—another big day, plus we'll discuss your deeds. But first, wash your clothes and take a hot shower. You're malodorous."

"Which means?" I asked tentatively.

"It means you stink so bad I may send you through the car wash!"

As Patch surfaced and showed off his putrid green tongue, for once I couldn't argue.

CHAPTER 11

"You're something else!" Kip cooed, stroking Patch under his puppy chin. "Bub, where'd you find this canine cutie?" she asked. My cheeks flushed, probably beet red. I knew she wasn't cooing at me exactly, but her bright smile delighted me, even though the sweet voice was meant for Patch.

"I got him at the um . . . pet store." Not sure how much to reveal, I felt uneasy about how I'd convinced the kind lady to give him up.

"Really? The pet store on Main Street?" Kip crinkled her nose and stared into my eyes. "He's adorable but kinda stinky, Bub. And what's that green stuff on your peach fuzz?"

Now my face was definitely deep red. I should have listened to Wahoo and taken a shower right away. "Something gross. Think I'd better change," I informed and took a step back so Kip wouldn't pass out from my dumpster cologne.

She nodded, and I jogged off to take a shower and change to an outfit in my overnight bag. When I returned, she was towel-drying Patch, who looked content in her arms. Not to be outdone, Hercules jealously yipped from the corner.

"Thanks for cleaning him up, Kip," I said.

"No problem," she replied as Patch let out a puppy yawn.

She handed over the sleepy pooch, and I gently escorted him to the RSS area designated for pets.

Strolling past a menagerie of fish bowls, parrot cages, and dog kennels, I found an empty one and placed Patch carefully inside. "Here you go, little prince. Soon you'll meet Howie who'll be your master."

I tucked the pet store lady's shawl in around Patch to keep him toasty until Christmas Eve. Patch snuggled in, and as I shut the kennel, twelve loud chimes rang from the nearby church clock tower—midnight.

A reminder that high noon was only twelve hours away, and I was out of commission until sunrise. I'd learned my lesson about walking around at night flush with cash. Thank the stars for Wahoo's rescue mission.

I surveyed the main warehouse area, dimmer than usual. Mr. Mabrey's office was dark, so the larger-than-life man actually left his office once in a while. Then I noticed the myriad of sleeping bags full of snoring Stocklings, with Jett leading the chorus, their heads and arms protruding from the bags. After stumbling around, I found an empty one with two envelopes marked BUB on the pillow. Wahoo's stamp was everywhere inside RSS.

I slid into the generous bag and got comfy. The envelopes had to be my other two Santa letters. Bathed in the glow of fairy lights, I opened the next one to peek at my challenge. "Dear Santa," it began. I paused, musing that I was one strange Santa—no red suit or white beard or Christmas cheer at the moment. Continuing:

"My name is Junie. Me and my mom need size small winter sweaters." Not too extreme, at least. Except that I knew zero about girls' sweaters.

Just then, Kip, cradling Hercules, tiptoed over to a sleeping bag near mine. Hercules crawled into the bag, and she climbed in next to him. Kip's gardenia scent was tantalizing.

"Find your other letters?" Kip whispered. "By the way, I think peach fuzz is cute."

Blushing again, I nodded. "Well, thanks. Uh, I need two girls' sweaters. Any ideas?"

She shrugged. "Be creative, Bub," Kip said through a yawn. "I remember my first golden deed."

I pulled the warm bag up around my neck. "How'd you do it?" I prodded, eager to know.

"My letter was from a little girl named Ellory, who'd never had a real Christmas tree or Santa presents before. She thought she hadn't been good enough, but really her grandma had been sick and just couldn't afford it." Kip's eyes moistened as Hercules snuggled up closer to her.

I swallowed hard and instantly thought of our Kitchen Kitty. It was low on funds, but at least Mom still got out the Christmas plates and decorations, and I knew there would be something under the tree—even if not a certain bike.

"Anyway," Kip continued, "I couldn't afford to buy a tree, so I talked to my parents, and they agreed I could bring our tree and some of my presents to her house. With her grandma's okay, after Ellory was asleep on Christmas Eve, we took everything over and set it up in her living room. My mom even helped me bake Santa cookies."

"Wow!" was all I could think of to say. It reminded me of the boy who'd gifted me his coin for the pawn shop. Kip had basically given away her own Christmas morning.

"You should've seen Ellory's face the next day," Kip said dreamily. "Her grandma sent pictures; she was beyond excited. It was *golden*."

I gazed at Kip, her eyes fluttering closed in the dim light. One thing for sure—she was resting easier than I was. Even though I'd showered and left my garbage-scented sweater in the washing machine, I wondered if my first good deed was what stank the most.

* * *

After nightmaring about the Red Phantom chasing me endlessly, I awoke to the sounds of bubbling and gurgling. "Huh? Wha—?" After a few restless hours of sleep, I had forgotten my whereabouts. But then I recalled sleeping under the RSS roof, the bazaar of bizarre, where anything goes. Stalling, I kept my eyes shut and played possum for another ten minutes.

"Morning, Mister Bub," Kip greeted. "Up and at 'em!"

Opening scratchy eyes, I stretched out my arms before realizing that a steaming mug of cocoa was being handed to me. I glanced around and saw the other Stocklings had left their bags also, and someone had wheeled the Drink-o-nator into the middle of the room.

"Umm," I said, sipping the drink. Kip also handed me a break-fast burrito that I wolfed down.

"While you were snoozing, Austin called you 'Sleeping Ugly.'" We laughed. "Oh, you might need this," she added, offering my freshly washed sweater. "Wahoo cleaned it—three washings."

"Thanks!" I said, hopping along in my sleeping bag before slipping out of it and donning the sweater. "What time is it?" I retrieved my boots, which I'd left by the door.

"Almost nine o'clock. Where are you going?"

A good question, one I had to answer fast. Ladies' sweaters . . . not my usual deal. Mr. Dixon's promised gift at Clarke's Department Store came to mind, but I wanted that kept close to the vest. Kip was staring at me expectantly over the top of her mug.

"Well, to someplace warm and friendly," I said even as I realized it myself. She had gotten help with her golden deed—so could I. In panic mode, I guzzled my cocoa and hustled out.

* * *

Junie's wish was simple enough, but Wahoo's ticking clock had really put the clamps on. In heavy traffic, it had taken me forever to walk home, leaving no time for a backup plan if Mom fell through. But she never fell through.

As I squelched up the path, Dad popped his head out of the garage. "Bub? Uh, you're home early. Or, wait, do I mean . . . you're home late?"

"It was that sleepover, Dad, remember?"

"Oh, right," he murmured as his head slipped back inside to whatever he was tinkering with.

"Mom! Mom? Are you home?" I called out, kicking off my boots. Thankfully, I'd caught her on break before the next shift.

"What is it, Bub? How was your sleepover?" Mom's voice trailed from upstairs.

"Oh, yeah, fun. Like being at work on night shift," I said with a roll of my eyes. "Mom, I need a big, huge, massive favor!" I begged, my tongue outracing my brain.

Taking the stairs two at a time, I rounded the top of the bannister and headed toward the master bedroom. "Cut to the chase, Bub. I'm on my lunch break."

"It won't take a second," I said, finding Mom in front of the mirror, brushing her hair. "I just need two sweaters."

"What do you mean? Check your closet; I'm sure there's a few clean ones in there. You look spiffy in that grey turtleneck."

"Thanks. Uh, I need . . . female sweaters."

Mom raised her eyebrow ever so slightly. "For you?"

"No," I said, shaking my head.

"For a girl?"

"Yes, for a girl. And her mom."

"Bub, do you have a private girlfriend you've been keeping from us? Are you ashamed of your own family?" Mom huffed and puffed, crossing her arms.

How could I wiggle out of this one?

"It's nothing like that. It's sort of a . . . secret Santa from me to the girl. Get it?" I felt my cheeks warming. The gift wasn't for Kip, but I realized it would be nice to give her one too.

"Think I see," Mom said, finishing her hair. "And you need one for the mother as well?"

"It's kind of a package deal—sweaters for both, and that equals one gift, by the game rules."

"What game rules? It sounds like Santa Monopoly. And what does Bub Olney get out of this?" she asked, suspicious. How did she do it? Mom's x-ray vision always saw through me.

"Well, it helps me at work, that's all. It's a mission I have to do."

"Mission impossible, huh. Are you play acting?"

"Honest! It's like a scavenger hunt where I find gifts for needy kids. All for charity." My voice cracked, and I cleared my throat. "And I get promoted when I nail everything on the list. Now I'm just a rookie and unranked." I was losing her. She stared blankly at me. "So . . . will you help me?" I pleaded, trying to keep my cool. "Christmas spirit?"

She eventually nodded—mothers always do—and I breathed a long sigh of relief. "You're sublime, Mom."

"Thanks, that's nice. They're in the top—"

Before she could say more, I'd opened the closet to find her sweater box. "Take two, but leave me the pink from Dad. You know I've worn them once or twice?" she told me.

"That's okay. Junie and her mom will absolutely love 'em." I lifted off the lid and pulled out two wool cardigans, noticing Chad's hidden Santa books still inside the box. Tucking the purple and green sweaters under my arm, I kissed Mom's cheek.

"How do you know they'll even fit?" she asked, still skeptical.

"They're perfect—I'm an expert," I said. "Gotta run now!" Mom was shaking her head as I dashed out the door.

Fortunately, she'd been a kid once and still understood our wacky brain circuits.

Fifteen minutes later, I could hear time ticking down—either my own heartbeat or the clock tower looming above as I entered RSS. It was 10:15 a.m., and I had yet to open the third envelope. Deadline: under two hours and counting.

"Sweaters for Junie!" I shouted, placing them folded onto Jett's shelves. I could hear Patch barking nearby, responding to my voice. Howie was one lucky kid.

Wahoo appeared, hearing my commotion. "Impressive, Bub."

"Yeah. Two down, one deed to go. By the way, thanks again for saving me last night." I still couldn't believe her karate prowess—a punkster Wonder Woman.

"Glad to assist. So how do you feel today?" Wahoo asked, eyeing me closely.

"Pretty good." Why was she staring at me like that? "I, uh, guess I'm skilled at using my wits to perform these deeds . . . like a game," I offered, uncertain what else to add.

Wahoo paused before answering. "Indeed, you're clever, and for that I commend you. But you won't be known in life for your words—you'll be known for your works, your *deeds*. Are any of yours to date golden?"

Her comments froze me. Golden? Maybe not as golden as Kip's, but. . . .

I found myself staring at Wahoo's shoes, unable to meet her gaze. All the excitement of finishing two deeds had crumbled. Finding the gifts was my doing, but Mom and the pet shop lady had selflessly given them to me. It was *their* sacrifice, not mine.

Just like the kid at the pawn shop who'd offered his treasure without thinking twice.

Wahoo wondered how I felt about the first two deeds. Easy—I felt sickened to the core . . . unworthy of a Corey. Then I remembered the clock was still ticking, and thankfully so was I.

One last chance to be golden.

CHAPTER 12

With only ninety minutes to go, I ripped open the last letter. My eyes scanned the first sentence, and my heart sank. "A computer? A freaking computer," I muttered.

Reading it over again didn't change the fact that I needed to conjure up a computer from thin air. A nine-year-old boy named Joshua had written: "Dear Santa, my folks own a small bakery and need a computer real bad."

How could I pull this one out of the bag? And in little over an hour? Not to mention, I had to make this deed golden or I'd be out of a job. A puppy and sweaters were child's play compared to a (working) computer. For the cost of a single desktop, I could've bought a dozen puppies or sweaters. What if I could borrow Austin's supercomputer and pay him back as an adult? No, that didn't sound golden or even legal. I had to make this miracle happen without cheating or acting. It had to be the real deal—a selfless act.

I was in unfamiliar territory.

Suddenly, the $500 in my pocket made itself known by wedging against my thigh. But that was my entire fortune; without it, I had nothing, and the Crusher was lost. There had to be some other way.

I thought about the ancient PC that Dad kept in the garage for parts, even considered getting Mom in the loop again, but rejected both ideas. She had already donated her sweaters, and his open computer had wires more tangled than Einstein's hair.

Reviewing the letter in hand, I realized that Joshua's mailing address was just two blocks away. The Hungry Amigo Bakery—a place I knew all too well for its scrumptious apple empanadas. My stomach was gurgling, and curiosity was calling, so I decided to first meet the kid to map out a game plan. Maybe they only needed a PC for bookkeeping, so a fancy calculator would fit the bill instead?

As the clock tower kept ticking away, I hightailed it to the bakery. The sombrero-wearing character on the sign grinned back at me as I approached the window display, filled with an array of baked goods. And there, front and center, restocking the holiday treats, was the boy from outside the pawn shop! The one who had given me—a total stranger—his prized coin. It couldn't be, yet it had to be.

This was *Joshua.*

Joshua turned slowly, noticing a hovering figure outside of the bakery. He smiled warmly at me, a glimmer of recognition in his eyes. "Hello!" he greeted, his voice muffled behind the glass.

"Hello, Joshua," I said. The boy looked puzzled that I knew his name, but continued smiling. As did I, grinning from ear to ear. Like a Rubik's Cube when the squares start lining up, suddenly I knew what had to be done. And fast.

I gestured toward the door of the bakery, and Joshua set down

110

his basket of muffins to come greet me. "You again . . ." This time he was wearing one red and one black stocking.

Of course he was.

"My name is Bub. Thanks for being kind at the pawn shop, Josh. I appreciate it, but I've come to return your money. It's a lot."

Joshua immediately shook his head. "No thanks, Bub. The coin was a gift. The money is yours, amigo. I don't even care if it's a hundred dollars."

If he only knew. . . .

Yes, it had been a gift; now I had the chance to give Joshua and family one in return. "A good deed outshines the sun, Josh. Merry Christmas—hope your wishes come true."

Before I could turn and leave, Joshua grabbed my sleeve. "Wait a minute, Bub," he urged. "Mama just cooked a fresh batch of empanadas. You seem like you could use one."

Indeed, I was a hungry amigo and probably looking a little worse for wear. My mouth was watering at the thought of the apple delight. Joshua slipped into the rear of the bakery and returned with a steaming empanada wrapped in foil.

"We'll meet again," I vowed, blowing on the pastry to cool it down. Waving good-bye, I gobbled down the treat on my jog back to RSS. After finding Joshua and realizing his identity, it was as if time stood still. Momentarily, I'd forgotten about my quest, and now I might miss the final countdown.

After arriving breathless and wiping crumbs from my lips, I observed both hands of the clock reaching skyward. It began to chime—high noon!

I was seconds late . . . the story of my life. But it didn't seem to matter anymore. Even if I lost my job at RSS, I could still perform a good deed for Joshua.

I listened to the last few chimes, enjoying the melody, standing on the doorstep of RSS and soaking in the day—snow-covered trees, clear blue sky, and the smell of chestnuts roasting. Behind me, the ornamental door swung open, and Wahoo appeared like magic. "Well, look what the cat dragged in!" she teased, standing barely in the sunlight.

"I'm late, Wahoo."

"Oh, ignore that old clock. It's at least a minute fast; rumor is there's a crow's nest in it."

I snapped to attention. "I'm not late?" We stood talking in the entryway.

"You're on time, by the skin of your teeth. Now where's the gift for your last deed?"

"Right here," I said, removing the $500 from my pocket. "I'd like to buy a new computer from RSS inventory, please."

"Isn't that your savings for the bike you covet?" Wahoo asked gingerly.

I shrugged and nodded.

Wahoo collected the $500 from my outstretched hand and declared: "Sold to the young man with the crew cut—one spanking-new RSS brand PC with all fine bells and whistles."

Our handshake sealed the deal.

"Joshua will receive the computer plus a free printer, with red

112

bow on top, on Christmas morning. RSS delivery goes 24/7 on Christmas."

"It's for his family," I explained. "They run the bakery over there," I added with a nod in the direction of The Hungry Amigo Bakery.

"Anything mouthwatering?" she asked, licking her lips.

"You kidding? Their apple empanadas rule the universe."

Wahoo flipped open her notepad and swished her pink feather quill back and forth, making a quick, invisible note. "Duly noted for my sweet tooth. Thanks, Bub." She handed me back $200.

"What's this?"

"Stockling discount for weekend warriors. Computer's yours for three hundred," she offered.

I looked down at the bonus $200 cash. "*Stockling* discount? Does that mean—"

"You completed the deeds. Now we just need to complete the ceremony."

Wahoo finally allowed me to cross the threshold into the warmth of the warehouse, and I quickly followed her through the tunnel—Red Phantom nowhere in sight. Wahoo brought me forward and whistled for all to gather.

Like a fire drill, everyone except Mr. Mabrey assembled in a flash.

"Well, Bub did it," Wahoo stated simply. The crowd of Stock-lings delivered uproarious applause with Coreys celebrating the loudest. Wahoo held up both thumbs as—due to the excitement? —her face had turned sunburn red.

Speaking of that color—I was told to reverse my right stocking to red, which I did, and the room erupted further. Even Hercules yapped as Patch joined in from a distance. I proudly admired the special pair of stockings that I'd earned.

"Having undergone training and needing a nudge or two along the way, blah blah blah, welcome to Stocklinghood as an official S3!" Wahoo announced. "So, Bub, how do you feel?"

Without worrying over everyone's reaction, not my usual, the words flowed as I placed my hand over my chest. "I feel . . . *lit up inside* . . . right here." Wahoo and all of the Stocklings nodded and placed their hands over hearts in turn.

And it was the truth, as if I'd gone back in time to recapture some long lost feelings . . . indescribable.

"You've only scratched the surface, Bub," Wahoo said. "If you've got the chops to make S2, it will open new doors including the chance to meet S1."

My eyes bugged. "S1? The real Santa? This is reality, not fantasy. Impossible."

"Is it? Now hear me: If you open your heart and mind to it, magic will reach out and tap you on the shoulder," she retorted before walking on. "It already has . . . look around you."

As the other Stocklings went back to work, Kip gave my arm a gentle squeeze. "Congrats, Bub," she whispered. "Herc and I knew you could do it."

We made small talk until she turned and headed for the elevator. My dangling arm still tingled from her touch.

Wahoo returned from Mr. Mabrey's office. As usual, her sunny disposition lit up the room, despite the shadowy recesses of RSS, which she rarely seemed to leave. Approaching me, she disclosed: "Hot off the press! We think you've earned something more, Bub."

We? I glanced over at Mr. Mabrey, behind the desk in his glass-walled office. This time he was writing—with a red feather quill, of course—on a long stretch of parchment. It occurred to me that I'd never seen him leave or even catch a drink from the break room. Bottom line: No sane human could resist the tasty beverages served at RSS. However, I knew he slipped away at night—or, at least he had on the night of the sleepover. So, he was either real deal Santa who used magic to transport back and forth to the North Pole . . . or a state of the art cyborg . . . or a white-bearded alien species on the prowl? Now I was really losing it.

As my mind swirled, I knew I had to get back on track. What did my bosses think I'd earned, beyond the rank of S3? I was so drained from my mad race for sweaters and a computer—not to mention green-tongued puppy escapades—that this new offer barely registered.

I needed sleep and serious time with the Drink-o-nator.

Wahoo gestured and bowed toward the Crimson Crusher in the center of the warehouse. If she was offering me a chance to sit on it, then she had no idea I'd been there, done that. Sneaky me had even ridden the Crusher in circles around the spooky warehouse.

"I've earned . . . a ride?" I asked. Then it dawned on me. The bike was sitting there on a silver platter. Could it be that simple? Was she finally mine?

"I informed Mr. Mabrey of your golden deed, and he's approved loaning the Cruiser to you."

"Loaning?" My heart skipped a beat. It was as close to owning as I might ever get, especially since the Joshua gift had nearly wiped out my savings with no chance at auction. "That's just—wow! Thank you," I managed to say.

"Enjoy the moment," she replied, strolling away.

I rushed to catch up with her. "Are you sure I can't offer you back the $200, plus any wages, to make her all mine? Officially?" I had to take the chance, maybe my last one.

"Sorry, Bub. Permanent loan is as good as it gets," she said, smiling. As her offer filtered through, I saw the light: *permanent loan.* Better to settle for riding a real bike that I didn't own, than to dream about a bike I'd never ride. Bottom line: dream fulfilled!

My adrenaline surged. Last roadblock removed—now I was getting ready to bask in every windblown moment.

As Wahoo waved to me excitedly, I grasped the handlebars and wheeled my Crimson Crusher to the loading bay elevator in the rear of the warehouse. I had never been up there, but thankfully only one red button was in sight. Even I could punch that . . . then industrial steel doors rolled up to reveal a blustery wonderland beckoning me.

Crimson Crusher vs. Old Man Winter . . . the day the wind met its match.

We went everywhere: looping around the park, riding parallel with the train tracks on the outskirts of town; weaving down streets in Sean's neighborhood; doing jumps off slopes and fallen logs in the forest; and then up and down Main Street like I was driving the best float in the parade! The tires were cutting deftly through the slush, and she held her own on the icy patches too. After a time, I felt saddle sore, but I was determined not to use that kickstand until it was too dark or my fingers were too frozen to hold on another second. . . .

It was a victory sweeter than any empanada.

CHAPTER 13

Skidding to a stop in front of Grant's Bike Boutique, I was reminded how much life had changed in such a short time. Here I was, atop the legendary Crusher, the glass pane no longer separating us. She was mine at last, or as close as I'd ever get.

I pedaled off, gaining momentum, heading back for the woods. Near the end of the block, suddenly two meaty hands slammed onto my handlebars, yanking them to a standstill . . . like hitting a boulder! I almost flew head over heels and saw red flash in front of my eyes. It was the hockey-shirted teen who'd tried to rob me outside the pet store! He was glaring at me with a bruised face, but my defender was nowhere in sight. And the thug had a savage look that said he knew it.

He had me right where he wanted.

"Nice bike, kid. You spent all your cash, I see?" he sneered with an appraising glance at the Crusher. "Guess I'll take this prize instead." This time around he held out a wooden baton menacingly.

"No chance!" I growled, fire in my belly. I'd come so far, achieved so much. I wasn't about to let this bully steal what I'd rightfully earned. Not without a fight. . . .

I quickly pushed off him, wrenching the handlebars from his hands, and slicing over his foot with both tires! He let out an awful yelp, like I'd crushed bones. Then I turned tail and raced off before he could grab me.

Instantly, he chased after me, half-hobbling, his face as red as his shirt. A powerful whack to the back tire from his baton knocked me sideways and disoriented. I quickly steered opposite, trying to correct course, but the Crusher fishtailed and spun out. Before I knew it, I'd turned completely around and was sliding backward while facing the mugger.

Time slowed. As the bike continued rotating, a darker red form raced into view . . . moving at high speed and toward my assailant. Bullseye! I heard a bonk and a bang as someone slammed into me, then silence and darkness for what must have been mere seconds, before bright light interposed. When I opened my eyes—woozy—I was still upright and the bike had completed one more 180-degree circle. As all came into focus, I discovered that both figures had vanished. The sound of splintering wood put me on high alert.

Where did they go? I searched around, puzzled. The only clue was footprints in the snow, similar in size to the puddles inside RSS, and the drag marks of another pair of boots alongside. Then both sets of prints disappeared into a slush pile beside an old dumpster. On top was a split baton snapped in two by someone with inhuman strength.

Thump! Something inside the large, metal container banged against the lid. "Help! Let me outta here!" yelled the imprisoned brute.

As the lid slowly creaked up, I took off, steering the bike for home. But wait . . . I spotted the darker hue of red—my rescuer—hustling between buildings and down an alleyway! He wasn't just a phantom figment of my imagination.

I couldn't let him disappear again without knowing his identity and why he kept crossing my path. Before giving chase, though, I had one more task. Turning back to the dumpster, I slammed a fist on the lid as I sped by, shutting it onto huge, splayed fingers prying it upward. When the teen groaned and turned silent, I knew he was out of action.

I'm not afraid of you anymore, I thought.

Instead, I was more intrigued by the mysterious stranger leaving the scene. I could barely keep up, even with my Crusher, as the trailing edge of a red cloak slipped around another corner and onto a residential street. I braked and darted my eyes around—nothing. . . .

Wait, *there*. Another fleeting glimpse of red. When I got close enough to see them, footprints led up a garden path to a lonely, ramshackle house, overgrown with thickets. I pulled the bike to the curb just in time to catch the red form dipping inside a storm shelter door next to the deserted house. The door shut with a rusty creak.

Now what?

Scratching my head through my hat, I shivered in the freezing wind. Who was he and why did he live in an abandoned building? Was he a fugitive? Suddenly, thunder crashed and rumbled close by! I gazed upward at the rapidly darkening skies, just starting to unleash thundersnow—a rare lightning-laced blizzard. This was no time to be outside. As the hair on my neck bristled, I turned homeward toward safety, rest, and hopefully Mom's piping-hot cocoa. Enough danger for one day and maybe a lifetime. Later—if I got up my nerve—I might return with some kind of weapon and a chain lock for my bike.

After making note of the street name, Willow Drive, I fought through the blizzard to follow back roads into my snowbound driveway. Reaching for the garage door handle, I almost jumped out of my skin as it abruptly clattered upward!

Dad emerged, hobbling on one crutch only. "Hey, Bub, where are you going?" he challenged.

"Uh, nowhere." He wasn't usually so protective of his garage and workshop area, but I probably should've checked with him first. "Just thought I could park my bike in the garage—thunder-snow tonight," I said, trying to read the odd expression on his face.

"Hmm, might be a problem, not much room," he explained, checking out the shiny Crusher. "It's a magnificent machine. But won't you miss your old bike? Hey, I know she's rough around the edges and has seen better days, but some elbow grease could fix her. Where did you—"

"Just a loaner from work," I replied, cutting him off.

Dad promptly relaxed. "Oh, I see. Then why don't you park her in the house? The garage isn't exactly Fort Knox. Since she belongs to your bosses, let's treat her like family."

"Really? In the house? Thanks, Dad, that would be brilliant."

"Sure. Wipe her down and lean her in the entryway beside the shoe rack. Just like a horse, huh? She'll be safe, since no thief could stand my smelly boots!"

We laughed heartily as I maneuvered my cycle up the front steps, and Dad grabbed towels from the entryway closet. Together we cleaned and dried her to perfection. "Welcome to my kingdom, Queen Crusher," I addressed my royal ride with a bow, rolling her tires across the threshold. Moreover, I was feeling good vibes from my father; maybe his leg was healing and he was pulling out of his funk.

"They must be happy with your work over there, Bub. A company car—well, company cycle—is one terrific perk."

"Yeah, guess I'm in the club now, or 'society' as they say. Don't worry; it's a good place." Then I heard footsteps on the stairs . . . my disillusioned little brother.

Chad had been silent, standing at the foot of the staircase, staring at the Crusher. Stone-faced, he finally spoke. "Very nice. Guess you got your dream bike for Christmas."

"Hey, I wish—it's just a loaner," I fibbed again, avoiding the word "permanent" and trying to avoid his envy. "Bet you'll get something cool under the tree," I said, despite knowing the Kitchen Kitty was starving.

"Yeah, I'm sure," Chad muttered, wandering into the kitchen with hunched shoulders.

What could I do? Tomorrow would be Christmas Eve, a magical day, yet Chad was acting like his holiday spirit was already crushed. And I knew it wasn't just about gifts; he was far less selfish than I'd ever been. No, it was as if the magic of the season had evaporated. Maybe Wahoo and the Stocklings could revitalize him, but that was down the road. As I racked my brain for ideas, I couldn't help doubting my own doubts— could S1 actually exist? If so, it would rekindle the flame in Chad. Yet common sense dictated that a living, breathing Santa was impossible. Then I recalled Wahoo's intriguing words: "If you open your heart and mind to it . . ."

Maybe logic doesn't exist in the Santa zone.

At dinner no one mentioned Christmas as we made small talk and feasted on Mom's holiday casserole. Afterward I showered and changed before the mirror steamed up, then crashed into bed. As I sank into the cushy mattress, a master plan started hatching in my head. It could work, but I'd have to forego exploring the house on Willow Drive until later and arrive early at RSS to discuss the plan with Wahoo.

Quickly, deep sleep embraced me. And the ghostly moonbeams spilling into the room spotlighted my dreamscape . . . a troupe of red stockings prancing before me, playing games, then scurrying up the wall and high-stepping across the green stucco ceiling.

CHAPTER 14

'Twas the day before Christmas and all through the house—I was more excited than a cat with a mouse! But my family needed fine-tuning: Chad had adopted my recent humbugness; Mom looked frazzled as she rushed out for her diner shift; and Dad was bored like a star quarterback riding the bench. And yet there I was, smiling and eager to work, because this was the day when all the magic happened. Yes, I said it. *Magic*. Not that I'd completely surrendered my brain to the cult of Santa marvel, but there was definitely something in the air!

Something contagious, something wondrous.

Yes, even shoveling the mountains of sidewalk snow was bearable. And riding the Crimson Crusher down empty streets as the sun burst over the horizon was an added bonus of early rising. I wanted to beat the other Coreys so I could snatch a moment of privacy with Wahoo before the madness kicked off. It promised to be a hectic day of organizing and boxing gifts, checking the list twice (per RSS rules), and getting final deliveries into perfect order for shipping. For the past several days, a fleet of FedEx trucks had descended upon our warehouse, loading up to start ferrying gifts to countless sites across North America. As one of the main headquarters, we had to be a well-oiled machine, guaranteeing delivery to exhilarated kids in time for Christmas Day surprises.

Whew! I was breathless just thinking about it. Or perhaps the icy morning air had stolen my breath as I pedaled in fast and skidded the last fifty feet. Leaning the Crusher in the long, dark corridor, I squeezed through the doorway and glanced around. Excellent—I'd managed to beat the morning rush.

"Bub—welcome, early bird, forget the worm," Wahoo greeted, appearing from behind a shelving unit. Checking the Candy Cane Clock, she added, "Well, there's plenty to do, so—"

"Actually, could we step into your office for a sec?" I asked, cutting her off. "I've got a plan to run by you. If that's okay?"

"Indubitably. Let's rock, Sherlock."

We had all the details ironed out by the time Kip and crew were hanging up their coats. "What was that about?" Kip probed, her bright smile welcoming.

"Nothing really, just talking to Wahoo about my, you know, Christmas wish list."

She nodded as Hercules yapped and popped his inquisitive head from her backpack. "That's cool, but only if you've got me something too . . . like a pony with a big red ribbon."

My mouth dropped open. "You? I mean, yeah, I could get you something, Kip. Because we're coworkers, right? Friends?"

She cracked a grin. "I'm horsing around, silly. Trust me, your friendship is gift enough."

"Oh. Well, how 'bout a Christmas cocoa right now?" I said,

seeking an excuse to make a fast exit. Although I'd talked to girls at school before, nothing had prepared me for Kip. She was just so . . . well, special. And she was opening up to me more and more.

"Sounds delish. Thanks, Bub."

I wandered off to the break room. While waiting to fill two mugs with frothy cocoa, I stared up at the pictures hung around the room. Wahoo had said they were old black-and-whites of Mabrey family Christmases . . . including him and his brother operating a train set, opening presents, and the Mabrey clan in pj's decorating their tree. A gleeful scene frozen in time.

Those images reminded me of Chad and myself, and I hoped my plan would bring holiday cheer to our family. Picking up the mugs, I headed back into the main area, where a busy hive of Stocklings stared at me like I had two heads.

"There he is; come join us, Bub," Wahoo said, waving me over.

"Wh-what's up, gang?" I asked, feeling awkward in the spotlight, worried that another big challenge was headed my way. Just my luck, some kid would crave a pet alligator or python or gorilla. I was allergic to all of those. In fact, I needed down time since RSS was jungle enough.

"Nothing you can't handle," Wahoo answered, wrinkling her nose.

This didn't look good. I handed off the mugs of hot chocolate to Kip and Austin, before returning to Wahoo's side. "Okay. Hit me with it," I jested. "Do I deliver all of these gifts on my own? Is that my next test? Am I promoted to S1 without a license? Ho ha ho!"

Nobody laughed or even smiled. Finally, Wahoo broke the silence. "Sounds like you don't know a good ho ho from a ha ha. We're not handing over the reins of the sleigh quite yet."

Sleigh? I'd been referring to the fleet of trucks. She couldn't possibly be serious, could she?

"First order of business," Wahoo continued. "Kudos, Bub. You're being promoted."

"Again?"

"Again."

"Why?"

"Why not!" She smiled. "Take it or leave it."

"Take it." I smiled back, now intrigued.

"Stupendous tremendous."

Wow, this was quite the Christmas totem pole I was climbing. At this rate, I'd have Mr. Mabrey's job by New Year's Day, I joked to myself, before turning serious. I knew by then Wahoo's decisions were well conceived, but it was still unbelievable. "You mean that I'm an actual S2?"

"S2 at age twelve, rounded off, the youngest one ever. You beat me by a week—that's not easy," Wahoo announced as the warehouse crowd started clapping.

"Not to be ungrateful, but how did I earn this?" One minute I was a Stockling in Training; now I'd ascended the ranks to S2— one level below the big guy himself. Talk about pressure. And I was too young for even a regular driver's license, let alone one for soaring sleighs!

"You're receiving this for golden deeds past and promised, if you catch my drift," Wahoo said with a wink. I got it, recalling our recent chat. "You may now reverse the black stocking to red."

I did and stood tall in my pair of red stockings as everyone clapped. "Thanks, Wahoo."

"Don't thank me," she corrected. "Mr. Mabrey made the final decision to promote you now. He can do that since he carries the rank of *S2 Royale* awarded for exemplary deeds."

And with that, the room let out a collective gasp. I wasn't sure why, until I slowly followed their eyes to Roy Mabrey's office. He was actually up from his desk, and the man himself was emerging in a scarlet-red jumpsuit! Should I have alerted the media?

He walked with definite purpose—eyes twinkling and smile radiant. There was no missing his fluffy, white beard and rosy cheeks.

"Indeed, I did," he said with a booming, friendly voice. "I'm very impressed with all of the Stocklings—including our newest member of the RSS family," Mr. Mabrey spoke with a regal air about him. "We're proud as punch to have you onboard, Master Olney. After being thrown into the deep end, you've learned to swim these chilling currents."

Master Olney? That sounded cooler than ice. My knees shaking, I tried to stay calm. "Thank you, sir." I was honored to meet him, knowing that he rarely spoke to anyone except Wahoo.

"From what I hear, your mind and heart are in the right place, young man. I've been keeping an eye on you and do believe that the stars aligned for you to join Red Stocking Society . . . your destiny. We do good by keeping alive a spirit beyond a legend. As empires rise and fall, St. Nick survives them all. Like him, bless his soul, we strive to cause an outbreak of giving."

Keeping an eye on me? Was it possible that Mr. Mabrey was the Red Phantom who'd been tracking me around the warehouse and in town? Looking the portly fellow over, I couldn't believe he was capable of the physical feats I'd witnessed. But, no question, he bore a striking resemblance to another jolly man in red: Mr. S. Claus.

Mr. Mabrey paused briefly, giving me time to speak, but words escaped me until I couldn't hold back the question. "Are you S1?" I blurted out. The room fell deathly quiet. I glanced at Wahoo, but she wouldn't make eye contact. "Sorry. What I mean is—"

"Patience," Mr. Mabrey interrupted. "All will be revealed soon." He brought forth an envelope and red box with white ribbon from behind his back, offering it with a flourish.

A gift? For me? "Thank you, sir. I'm honored. Um, what is it?"

Mr. Mabrey smiled, his white whiskers tickling his mouth. "Read the letter with delight and open the box tonight to experience S1 . . . *real Santa*! You have my word on it."

The real Santa? Was I dreaming again? The pinch test proved negative, not a dream. I gently shook the box, and it rattled.

Nothing alive inside, not even an elf.

"Merry Christmas!" Mr. Mabrey proclaimed, extending his arms to include everyone around us. "I feel like today is going to be productive and—also for Bub—reflective. Just don't be late; enjoy your fate!" And with that, the poet in red whisked back into his office, closed the door with a click, and the entire floor of Coreys, Fixers, and Hivers sprang to life and back to work.

Taking Mr. Mabrey at his word, I found my thoughts racing. Somehow the combination of circumstance, hard work, a bit of luck, and dash of heart had helped me arrive on this stage. And soon I would be privileged to meet the legendary, living Santa Claus.

If any of my skeptical friends got wind of this, forget it.

The next few hours were a kaleidoscope of colorful wrapping paper and ribbon. Jett operated the carousels of shelves; Austin clicked through lists of worthy children and addresses; Kip led the wrapping and gift flow to the dispatch area; and I fulfilled last-minute orders from Inventory.

By lunchtime, we were all exhausted and barely on schedule. But Wahoo seemed pleased as she studied the blank page on her pad, the pink feather fluttering in her hand. Everything seemed to be going according to plan—hers and mine. "Thank you all, I am proud!" she said with a nod.

Yet one thing kept nagging me. If Mr. Mabrey was neither S1 nor the mystery man, then who was the stranger haunting RSS and protecting me? Was it all a ruse so I'd let my guard down?

The answer awaited me on Willow Drive. And with the gifts piling high in the loading zone, I knew that our only remaining task was to monitor the trucks, or sleighs, or whatever would be carting them off. So, I asked Kip to cover for me while I ran an errand. No one, including Wahoo, knew what I was up to. I stowed Mr. Mabrey's gift box and letter in a secret place, slipped on my winter wear and rushed off down the tunnel, where the sturdy Crimson Crusher was waiting in the shadows. I felt like a mythical warrior of old riding his trusty steed into battle.

Off we went, racing along back streets as I pointed the handlebars in the direction of the derelict house. Bathed in cold sweat, I headed toward a showdown with an elusive Red Phantom.

Maybe I should have just stayed at the warehouse, warm and cozy. But after so many dead ends, curiosity was driving me to figure out this piece of the puzzle. As I rode closer to my destiny, trying to think positive, an old saying crept into my head: *Curiosity killed the cat!*

CHAPTER 15

Dark snow clouds above the rooftops of Willow Drive seemed foreboding as I chained my Crusher to the only strong rail attached to the rusty fence. The bike looked out of place, like the one shiny apple in a barrel of rotten fruit.

With a deep breath, I began trudging up the unshoveled pathway, wading in knee-high snow and feeling the winter chill in my bones. The decrepit old house appeared even creepier as I sluggishly approached. My eyes skittered over the gloomy exterior: grimy, mold-mottled walls; rain-rotted shutters; and metalwork encrusted with rust.

Welcome to the Roach Motel—holiday rates dirt cheap. I couldn't even rally a grin.

Why hadn't I brought along backup? Jett could smash any psychos with his cane or Kip could unleash Hercules on phantoms. And Wahoo could handle just about anything with her martial arts, human or otherwise. Instead, I was alone and jittery, my butterflies inside doing loop-the-loops. Just in case, I searched around for something to fend off an attack. And there it was—a broken branch from a snow-laden tree. Not exactly a lightsaber, but it would just have to do. Speaking of light, I suddenly realized I'd forgotten my flashlight.

Sometimes blind luck can save the day. *Why not today*, I thought.

Clutching the branch like a club, I creaked up the porch steps, fearing they might collapse any moment and drop me into some bottomless pit. But they held up, only bowing slightly. As bitter wind whistled eerily through the house, I noticed the porch was in worse shape than the stairs. My initial plan to enter through the front door was impossible, since it and the windows were boarded up.

I wondered if that was done to keep things out or in?

Plan B: I knew of another entrance—used by the red-cloaked figure when I'd followed him here. If I dared to enter. Carefully descending the porch steps, I waded through snow banks to the storm door where half-buried footprints were signs of life. I was in the right place . . . or maybe the wrong?

Only one way to find out.

I used the branch to pry open the door. "Hello?" I yelled, about to hoof it . . . but dead silence.

It was decision time. For some reason I was drawn to the Red Phantom like he was drawn to me. And for whatever purpose, he had rescued me more than once.

Shivering while taking one last look at the world, I plunged into the darkness. The dank, musty smell made me think I was inside the house basement, though I seemed to be veering away from the building itself. Sheltered from the cold, I stopped shivering and used the branch to guide me like a blind man, which I was. Thankfully, the dirt path provided sure footing as I placed a hand on the wall, feeling bricks, wet and slimy to the touch.

If anything nearby growled or hissed, I was ready to open up a can of adios amigos!

Then I saw a sliver of light up ahead, flickering like a candle, guiding me. Someone was here.

Watching.

Waiting?

A scuffle to the rear. I raised the branch, ready to swing at anything in motion. But the sound stopped suddenly, so I continued moving ahead, hoping it was a mouse and not a certain scarlet spook, enraged that I'd invaded his domain.

I crept onward with the light getting closer and closer, brighter and brighter. And now I could see light shining under what appeared to be a seamless stone wall. A trick door perhaps that concealed a hidden room? I could hardly breathe, my chest constricting with fear.

Wiping the slime onto my jeans and clutching the branch in a death grip, I sucked in one last breath and reached out to the wall in front of me. I gave it a hard push, and surprisingly the wall creaked open like a regular door. It wasn't locked? I scratched my head and dared to step inside, finding a flickering lantern dangling from a rafter.

Where was I? Who'd lit this lantern? And why was he hiding in this underground lair? I reached up and unhooked the lantern, trying to shed more light on the subject. As if answering my question, I turned around to discover a metal plaque screwed into the stone wall: RSS, Inc.

What? I was *inside* RSS!

I quickly glanced around. These stone walls resembled the tunnels tapering off the main corridor to the RSS warehouse. But how could this be? In my mind, I retraced my ride over to Willow Drive, trying to figure if I'd traveled a similar distance. In fact, I'd meandered up and down several back streets, while a direct path would've been shorter. Of course, a secret underground tunnel could bypass the winding roads and give someone a direct—and private—path into the RSS building.

This was a game changer.

Think.

Fast!

Just like Wahoo had said, the warehouse itself was actually underground, meaning these tunnels could easily be linked into that same grid. But if so, then who was the Red Phantom and what was his connection to RSS?

I shone the lantern down the tunnel, which had many off-shoots. Vigilant, I moved forward, feeling a bit calmer knowing that RSS and my friends were nearby. Nonetheless, I was still trapped in these catacombs with no clue of what lay ahead or how to escape if attacked.

My train of thought derailed when I heard another fleeting scuffle. Only it wasn't behind me this time; it was ahead of me. My heart in my throat, I proceeded slowly, frayed nerves shot.

Was someone baiting me? Had I been lured here by a criminal or psycho to kidnap me?

Trembling but determined, I pulled my jacket around the lantern to conceal the light and stared into the pitch-black darkness. Then another light flickered around the corner.

I tiptoed forward, hoping to surprise whatever lurked in the shadows, ready to swing the branch with force. There was a small doorway and another lit lantern on the wall straight ahead, illuminating a sort of mini-cave.

As I was about to peer inside for a closer look, suddenly I heard a whoosh as someone blew out the lantern flame! I instinctively lurched forward and off to the right, probing the darkness with my branch. "I've got a sword—I'll slice you to ribbons!" I yelled.

When I stepped one foot onto *nothing*, a deep voice uttered, "Freeze or die!" as a large hand clamped on my arm and pulled me backward! For a moment, my feet dangled in space, before stepping on firm ground and regaining traction. Petrified, with a galloping heart, I attempted to scream, but no sound escaped!

Gasping and struggling, I dropped the branch and lantern, then broke free. The lantern's glow revealed a deep pit that I'd barely escaped . . . and a stocky red figure who'd saved my life again?

"Th-thanks for saving me. Who are you?" I sputtered.

The figure turned around, revealing his majestic presence in all of its glory: long, red cloak with white fur frosting the collar; large, black leather belt with shiny golden buckle at the waist;

silvery-white beard; and those sparkling eyes, beneath a red hat with more white frosting around the brim. It was *Santa Claus*!

Rather, it was Mr. Mabrey dressed as Santa Claus.

"Mr. Mabrey! What are you doing here?" I stammered.

He stared blankly at me, clearly in actor mode and playing dress-up in his underground shock theater. Unless . . . could it be? Was he the real S1, after all?

The man opened a hidden door and led me into a room lit by twin lanterns. It was surprisingly homey. True, the walls were all stone with no windows—being underground—but there were creature comforts like a hanging mirror, mattress bed with quilt, rocking chair, and desk with writing materials. Somebody lived here.

Mr. Mabrey lived here!

"I don't know you," he stated in a kind voice, keeping up the charade.

"Sir, I met you today. You gave me a promotion and a gift, remember? Or are you in Santa mode right now?" I asked, remaining wary, hoping to avoid a Jekyll and Hyde scenario.

"Oh, that's not possible," he replied matter-of-factly. "I haven't met anyone in a long time, but I am Mr. Mabrey."

I shook my head, ready to rock if he rolled. "Uh, what do you mean?"

"I'm *Ray* Mabrey. You met my brother, Roy, who runs RSS, Inc. He's the rich one."

Ray and Roy! The brothers from the black-and-white pictures. "You're twins!" I gasped again. "But why are you hiding out down here? And dressed like Santa Claus? It's a little weird," I babbled before stopping myself.

"Don't you know what day it is, young man?"

"Well, sure. It's Christmas Eve."

"Exactly," he said with a blink of his now twinkling eyes.

"Just getting in the Christmas spirit, huh?" Was this guy cuckoo?

"Ho ho ho!" Ray Mabrey chuckled, not relieving my concerns.

"You, uh, don't think you're the real Santa, do you?"

"Well, in a way, I am . . . I was. I had been an S4—store Santa— for many years. That all changed when Macy's decided to hire a younger, 'cooler' version. They told me to hang up my suit. I gotta tell you, it about killed me. Sure, I worked the rest of the year, selling insurance, but my job always let me off for a month of full-time S4 work, and I lived for the season. Without being able to light up everyone's eyes at Christmas, I just couldn't cope." Tears welled up as he continued. "I was so ashamed. Look, you've seen RSS—remarkable and inspiring. How could I face Roy, knowing that I could no longer bring joy to kids? I'd let down the Mabrey name. After my wife passed on, I thought it best to exile myself from the holiday and family I love as self-punishment, rather than hang around and disappoint. I knew the layout of RSS, used to explore it lots, so it was easy to just disappear. I'll admit it's made me a bit crazy at times."

"So that's why Mr. Roy Mabrey spends so much time in his office . . . worried and wondering where you are. Your pictures are all over the break room. He must miss you a lot."

Ray stared at me and smiled. "It's time the phantom of the warehouse escaped from shadows to come home. Thank you, Bub."

"Wait a second, thought you didn't know me?"

"Not personally. But I've watched you from afar, heard your name bantered about, from the time you showed up. I could tell you had spirit and a big heart once you found it," Ray added with a wink.

"It was you, then? You saved my bacon all those times—like today?"

With a blush, Ray nodded. "Roy was always the intellect in the family and me the jock. Just looking out for Stocklings like you and him."

"Thank you. Were you a Stockling once too?"

He laughed. "No, that's a tough job. My skill is working with kids to brighten their day. I live to give. It's why I like to be close to the action, wander the building at night, see the new toys, even snatch food and drinks from the break room. Call me a friendly Bandersnitch who's a fellow chocoholic. Brings back happy memories of Roy and me working and playing together."

"Build new memories, then. I mean, look at you . . . seasonal threads, raring to go."

"All I need is an 'Unemployed Santa' sign to wear," he jested, striking a nifty pose.

"Nah," I countered. "There's always Santa work around Christmas, and you live to give."

"Indeed," Ray agreed, taking a lantern and leading the way. "Follow me, young man."

"Happily, sir. By the way, is the old house on Willow Drive where you and Roy grew up?"

"Yes, and it's connected to this secret tunnel system dug during the Civil War. Our favorite hideaway as kids. You're sharp, Bub, what I'd expect from an S2 prodigy."

"Thanks!"

"You're jolly welcome, young sir!"

As I struggled to keep up, Ray Mabrey's uproarious "Ho ho ho!" echoed throughout the weaving web of tunnels leading to RSS, Inc.

CHAPTER 16

We wound through the twisting tunnels to arrive at the warehouse's small entrance. I wondered if Ray could squeeze through, but showing Santa-worthy chimney skills, he sucked in his belly and forced himself past the door frame.

Once inside, he revealed a secret: The doorway was constructed of hard rubber with just enough give to allow kids and most adults through. Another RSS oddity meant to tease the mind.

It was getting late in the day, and the usual hustle and bustle had tapered into casual to-and-fro as Wahoo oversaw final details of the big pick-up. Our arrival brought everything to a sudden halt as the Stocklings' eyes turned to the impressive man in red behind me.

Wahoo whistled and dropped her pink feather to stare agog. "Stocklings, assemble—something *consequential!*"

Kip stepped forward, moving her mouth, yet no words escaped. Austin screeched the brakes on his chair, locking eyes on the familiar-looking fellow. Jett continued working, blissfully unaware.

"Send Bub to collect Winky Wizard dolls for Astrid and Ondine in Austin," he advised. Met with silence, he frowned. "Hello? Did you hear me, Kip?" Jett said louder, but still no response. "What's wrong with everyone, huh?" He extended his hand and touched goosebumps on Kip's bare arm. "C'mon, girl, you're acting like you've seen a ghost."

"Maybe I have . . ." Kip said softly.

At that moment, Mr. Mabrey hustled out of his office for the second time that day, clipboard in hand, ready to get the show on the road. He nodded briefly in passing at his brother, who was still standing on the welcome mat. "Ray . . ." Mr. Mabrey said distractedly and kept walking.

One step.

Two steps.

Three.

Then Roy Mabrey froze. Spinning around, he gaped at Ray, who was smiling back at his twin brother.

"Hi, Roy," Ray replied.

"You-you're alive!" Roy gasped.

I gazed around the room at the ashen faces. "Good surprise, huh?" I asked, but my coworkers were still too stunned to react.

"I guess I am," Ray nodded, poking himself. "Although I've been flitting around in shadows like a ghost, I am here—in the flesh, with a little bit of flab. I'm so sorry for worrying you."

Roy shouted, "Love ya, bro!" and closed the gap between them, giving Ray a huge bear hug. They double high-fived and crossed arms in a brotherly ritual, bringing shouts and whistles from around the room. The two men were twins in every way, except for Ray's slightly longer beard. If Ray hadn't been playing Santa, I couldn't have told them apart.

"I'm just glad you're all right and you're back. You are back, aren't you? For good?" Roy asked, breaking away from Ray to study him closely.

"Absolutely," Ray answered. "I've wallowed for long enough. Time to get back in the saddle—I mean sleigh. I'll explain everything later."

By this time all of the Stocklings had shown up and were awaiting expectantly.

Roy turned to the shocked staff. "I've found something I thought was lost forever . . . family." Roy placed an arm around his brother's shoulders. "Everyone, this is Ray, my long-lost brother. The *ghost* of Christmas past returns! Master Olney, you're a gentleman and a scholar."

I bowed slightly as everyone cheered. Not a dry eye in the room.

Walking around the warehouse floor, Ray shook each Stockling's hand, grinning with delight. He'd obviously missed socializing and being the center of attention. What agony he must have endured while hiding from people so long. That's when I brainstormed another gift to be the icing on the cake.

But could I pull it off in time?

"Bub, that's phenomenal, you're earning your stripes!" Wahoo said, tapping me on the arm.

"Thanks, Wahoo. Could I ask another favor?"

"Name it."

"I don't have a cell. May I use your land line?"

She nodded and didn't ask why. I smiled and slipped into her office as the Mabrey clan and Stocklings celebrated Roy belting out Jingle Bells on his saxophone.

I reached into my right pocket. Uh-oh, where was it? Sighing, I dug deeper . . . bingo. I pulled out a business card, grabbed the phone, and dialed. "Hello? Mr. Dixon? I hope you remember me, Bub Olney, from the street the other day. I grabbed your sleeve and—" I paused as he cut in. Mr. Dixon said he'd never forget and thanked me again before I got down to business. "Well, I'm wondering if we could talk about that store gift?" I explained what I needed and listened before answering: "Sir, thank you for this valuable gift."

* * *

Kneeling on my bedroom floor, I placed the gift box from Mr. Mabrey in front of me. From this angle, I could see the container under the bed where I'd stashed remaining cash. I knew there wasn't enough to officially own the Crusher, but it was okay. A bike was mere metal.

What could the gift be? The box wasn't heavy, nor did its rattle reveal any secrets within. But I knew what awaited me inside wouldn't be ordinary. Not RSS's style.

The handwritten card read: *To Bub: Open at eleven tonight, and you'll soon have Santa in sight! R. Mabrey.* It was 11:01 by the digital clock on my bedside table. I could hear Mom and Dad bumping around downstairs, switching off tree lights, making their way upstairs to bed.

With a deep breath, I lifted the lid to unveil the contents of the package. Typical of RSS, it was simple yet intriguing. There was a hand-drawn map to somewhere, a letter in Mr. Mabrey's handwriting, and an LED flashlight with cherry-red bulbs. Oh yeah, also a wrapped frame with label: *Picture of real S1, open me last to stun!*

Unbelievable. The secret of the S-Game would soon be mine.

I scratched my head, glanced at the map, then scanned the brief letter. It read: *Dear S2 (that's you): Do not take a nap, just follow the map.* Mr. Mabrey's sort of poetry had me riveted.

Studying the map, I recognized the destination—a small hill inside City Park, behind Main Street. One of my old stomping grounds. This was becoming curiouser and curiouser.

*Right on the stroke of midnight, illuminate your flashlight. Point to where it's starry, you will not be sorry. And when you are finally done, Santa magic will become **one**.*

Become *one*? Written in bold, that had to be important. Mr. Mabrey actually wanted me to sneak out on Christmas Eve, during the witching hour, to shine a flashlight into outer space. Leaving my warm room behind to climb a snowy hill at midnight to experience what exactly?

The complete unknown.

Sounded like a blast . . . no stopping now!

Grabbing the box and contents, I pulled on a coat, cracked the window ajar, and dropped the metal escape ladder. Careful not to slip, my boots soon crunched into the snowbank below.

Making a beeline for Main Street, I could see the top of the hill up ahead. It was a sizable mound in the center of the park, giving a panoramic view over the town and surrounding homes.

And on this clear-skied night, it was a perfect spot for star-gazing too.

I gazed up at the cosmos, glistening and glorious, wondering how my puny flashlight could possibly connect with anything out there? It would be just another blip in a galaxy of planets, moons, and shooting stars. I trudged past a familiar slide and swing set and kept moving. Close to midnight, I clambered up the snowy slopes of a hill that was carved with a crisscross of toboggan tracks.

Still holding the box, I struggled to get a grip with my boots as I neared the top. Every labored step, I could see more of the town's rooftops and smoking chimneys coming into view. It was one beautiful setting for a midnight surprise. But why was I here?

At the summit, I slumped to my knees, heavily winded. Removing the instructions again, I reread them: *Santa magic will become **one**.*

It still didn't make sense. I checked my watch: one minute and counting. I removed and examined the red LED flashlight, ordinary enough, except for the bold RSS logo imprinted on it. But these were RSS-designed lights—guaranteed to be radical.

With a shrug, I aimed the flashlight skyward and took a deep breath. Right at midnight, I clicked the button—unleashing the brightest, reddest beam I'd ever seen.

It was like a crimson bolt of lightning was firing from my flashlight. "Sweet!" I exclaimed.

Transfixed, I peered up and down at the dazzling red light, stretching into the heavens, going on forever. And that's when I noticed the *others*. To my left, to my right, some close, some far away—from other towns and cities—thousands of spindly, red columns, seemingly holding up the sky. A stunning sight.

Basking in the glow of red light warming my face, I felt connected to something marvelous and magical, that tugged at my heartstrings. Only I wouldn't learn until morning how true this really was.

After several minutes, the flashlights began to fade, then extinguish from the sky. Mine was one of the last to die out. I shook it several times and figured the massive power of the beam must have zapped the batteries.

Feeling zapped myself after a long day, I smiled and sat there for a while . . . reflecting, while gazing at the celestial light show. About to drift off, suddenly I snapped to and ripped opened the wrapped frame . . . revealing a mirror that reflected *my own face* with mouth agape and filled with wonder! Shocked beyond words to finally meet real S1, I couldn't quite grasp the meaning of it all.

At least not yet.

CHAPTER 17

I woke up the next morning—Christmas Day—grinning like a Cheshire cat. Lying in bed, I relived the majestic light show of red beams piercing the sky. Then I imagined the epic rides that RSS's deliveries must have taken to gift eager kids everywhere. Finally, I pondered the grand mystery that I was close to solving.

The magic of this special day colored everything.

I jumped out of bed. It had been billed as a meager material Christmas compared to other years, but maybe I could help put smiles on my family's faces.

If so, there was nothing I couldn't do.

Opening my bedroom door, I was startled to find Dad already awake and full speed ahead. "Merry Christmas, Bub!" he greeted. "Let's get Chad."

I could already hear Mom fiddling with kitchen chores downstairs, the familiar sights and sounds of Christmas Day.

Home sweet home.

"Sure. Merry Christmas, Dad! Hey, no crutches?" I asked, eyeing him with surprised delight. Recently, he'd seemed more like himself, and today he was standing on his own.

He grinned with thumbs up. "I'm just hoping to get Chad

back in the swing of things. He loves Christmas, and I won't let him miss his favorite holiday."

"Miss it?" Dad rapped on Chad's door.

No response.

"Well, mope through it," he said, before yelling: "Wake up, lazy bones. Time to rise and shine, Chad! Need you by the tree in five." Then he turned to me. "By the way, did you eat all the Santa cookies? I didn't nor did your mother."

"No, I never saw them—wish I had."

"Hmm . . . strange. See you by the tree." With that, he went downstairs, barely limping.

I ran through the bathroom, washing up, then knocked on Chad's door again. "C'mon, squirt, time's wasting! First a lecture, then we'll check if Santa came."

Chad stared at me with a grouchy face. "Yeah, right, and don't call me squirt!" he said curtly.

There was no crazed dash for breakfast today. Instead, Chad trudged behind me in pj's, his mood showing with every heavy tread. I couldn't help smiling; he had no idea what lay ahead.

In the family room, Dad stood with arms crossed, speaking volumes before opening his mouth. "Merry Christmas!" he said, turning on the radio to play soft holiday music in the background. Famished, I noticed the Santa cookie plate holding mere crumbs on the counter.

"Is it?" Chad asked, nodding to the pile of mainly small gifts. Both of us sat waiting for the Gettysburg Address.

"It is!" Dad retorted with certainty. "Let me remind you that

Christmas isn't just about receiving gifts. Sure, that's a fun part of it and maybe why you adored the holidays since you were a little boy," he said, looking at Chad. "You liked the magic of it all, until you started to question it," Dad continued, turning his attention to me. "But, really, it's all about sharing and giving to those we care about. And while we may not be wealthy, we are the luckiest family anywhere since we have each other. Material things come and go, my sons—unimportant. What counts are people who help us build something beyond rich bank accounts . . . rich *memories*."

Wow!

Dad's lectures often fell flat as a pancake, but this time Chad and I listened closely. At that point, Mom stepped in from the kitchen, bringing good scents and a tray of juices and coffee. "Well, hotshots, here's my present," she announced. "I got a huge ham as a Christmas bonus."

Her men clapped with ravenous glee.

Dad raised a finger in the air. "It's not about having the biggest ham either," he said firmly, before grinning. "But it keeps our stomachs content during this special day that might include scalloped potatoes and chocolate pecan pie?"

"I'll never tell. Just wait and see," Mom replied coyly.

Dad and I burst into grins as Chad raised his hand. "I wanna say I know how lucky I am—our family—and getting what I want isn't such a big deal. So, I'll try not to be too disappointed." Holding it in, he added: "So are we gonna open these puny gifts or what? I mean, it's Christmas!"

"After the prayer," Dad reminded. As we bowed our heads, he recited a heartful prayer. Then he tussled Chad's hair and nodded. "Good job, son. Now, Olneys, let's begin. Who's on first?"

Mom plopped herself down in the armchair, extending weary legs. "Mama me, I earned it!"

Smiling, Dad handed a small box from under the tree to Mom. "This is my thank-you for all that you do including our soon-to-be scrumptious Christmas feast." He gave her a big hug.

"I appreciate you too, more than ever," she said, untying the bow on the box and peeking inside. A notecard read: "Finally, I fixed the microwave and stereo, but the toaster is toast." Mom grinned and clapped. "Yea! More fast food plus I can play my Beatles albums again. Thank you, Hon. And about that toaster—I had a feeling." From behind her chair, she held up a new toaster wrapped in red ribbon! The rest of us stood, cheering. "Now would you pass that one to Chad?"

Blushing, Dad reached under the tree and handed Chad a square package. "What is it?" Chad asked, weighing the bulky gift in his hands.

"Something you should keep," Dad replied. "And never lose— no matter your age."

Chad tore off the paper to reveal his stack of well-read Christmas books that Mom had rescued. "Never lose my books?"

"What your father means is, never lose the spirit of the holidays," Mom interjected.

"Well, I might not ever read them again, but thanks anyway. Hey, I didn't forget you guys either," Chad said, lighting up and stepping into the hallway. He returned with a holiday basket of candies, fruit, and nuts.

"Chad, that looks delectable!" Mom exclaimed. "You didn't have to."

"Just a little something from my shoveling bucks. There's dark chocolate clusters for Bub—dark is healthier—and roasted pecans for Dad, even organic apples for you," he said proudly.

Mom licked her lips. "Yummy. And you're one of the apples of my eye."

Chad nodded, looking pleased.

Even Dad jumped in. "Thanks, son. You're so nutty."

Chad half-smiled at the puns, but I knew he was faking for their sakes. My little bro was still fixated on the Blue Beast.

"Okay, my turn, thanks for the clusters, bro," I chimed in. "First off, parent people, the Kitty looks fatter. Check it out." I located my pile of three gifts under the tree. Yesterday, I'd bought them with my S2 discount from RSS inventory, and Kip had even helped with wrapping.

Mom opened hers first. It was a new cardigan sweater, blue to match her eyes. She smiled at me. "Is this to replace the donation for your li'l galfriend?" she teased. I blew a raspberry at her, and she laughed. "Thank you, sweetie. Love it."

Dad opened his next—a bestseller fix-it book. "Hey, thanks, Bub!" he said while thumbing through it and earmarking pages. "With this I could become dangerous." The rest of us nodded.

Finally, I handed Chad his gift. He tore back the paper in one second flat. "New gloves?" he half-asked, half-stated.

"Yes. And they'll be useful for shoveling snow or riding a bike or whatever . . ." I'd already anticipated his response.

"What do you mean?" he quizzed. Our parents were equally puzzled.

I grinned knowingly. "They have special grips—should come in handy. Wanna go outside and see if it's easier to . . . ah . . . shovel? Fewer blisters, guaranteed."

Chad bit his lip but didn't frown. "Maybe later, Bub. Thanks."

"Oh, come on," I coaxed. "Just try 'em out."

"What're you up to, Bart Olney?" Mom asked, her eyes squinting. Sheesh, did she have to know every time I was fibbing?

I winked at her, trying to send a message. "Oh, all right," she relented. "Why don't we step outside a minute to enjoy our white Christmas?"

Dad shot Mom a strange look. "In the front yard?" he asked.

"No, back yard," I answered for her.

With that, Chad shrugged, and the Olney family—wrapped in winter wear over pj's—trooped out the back door, stepping onto the snow just as a cheerful sun peeked through the clouds. Chad still looked perplexed.

"You know what's weird, guys?" I went on. "I could've sworn I heard scuffling down here last night. Sounded like it was coming from there." I pointed toward one of the big boxwood hedges by the house. Leaning against it was Chad's snow shovel.

"Hope it's not a stowaway," Dad said, clueless to my plan. "An animal trying to get warm?"

"Snow's thicker behind the hedge, Chad—try shoveling with your new gloves," I suggested.

"Be careful," Mom warned as we approached the hedge. "You never know what might be lurking." Little did she know.

Keeping his game face on, Chad shot me a look and ducked behind the hedge as my parents stared. Suddenly, with a cry of jubilation, he rolled out the Blue Beast in all her gleaming glory!

"B-b-but, how?" Chad stuttered, pumping his fist victoriously.

"Yes, how?" Mom whispered, both confused and joyful. "Ron, did you . . .?"

"No!" Dad declared. "I promise it wasn't me."

"Bub?" Mom probed.

"Nope," I replied, technically correct, since the gift wasn't from me. "Like I have the money anyway . . . must be from Santa."

"Really!" Chad squeaked. "The bike is actually from Santa?"

Mom was crying but smiling through the tears. "Chad, it has to be Santa," she said with barely a glance in my direction. "Otherwise it's . . . impossible."

Chad turned his focus to me. "So, Santa's for real, Bub?"

This time I was ready. "There's no other explanation, bro, so figure it out for yourself. I do believe Santa wonder happened here. Don't forget this."

"Yesss!" Chad exclaimed, nodding in wide-eyed wonder.

Dad put his arm around Mom, and I beamed a triumphant smile.

"Bub, let's go for a ride!" Chad begged, admiring and clutching the Beast, as if to keep it from evaporating. The crystal-blue frame glistened in the morning sun.

"Oh, uh, well . . . remember the Crimson Crusher was just on loan," I sputtered. "I had to give her back to RSS since my holiday work is finished."

All of them swiveled their heads to stare at me.

"Let me get this straight," Dad said, scratching his head. "You had to return your super cycle, and now you don't have a bike at all?"

I nodded. "That about covers it." Except it didn't, really. During our private meeting, Wahoo had said the Crusher was officially mine—a perk of Stockling status. Then I'd taken my dream bike to Grant's and exchanged her for Chad's dream instead. The owner was sworn to secrecy.

All in a day's work as an S2—making magic happen.

Dad's face cracked into a smile. "You really need to open the garage, Bub."

"Huh, okay." Did Dad have something up his sleeve too? Bemused, I pulled on the garage door handle, realizing his little workshop had been off limits lately. What had he been working on in there?

A shaft of light from the open doorway showcased his gift for me—my old *bicycle*, lovingly restored and painted amber! She looked as good as new. "Dad, it's a masterpiece!"

He chuckled. "You thought she was ready for the garbage heap, so I raided that junkyard by the railroad tracks. Found some bits and pieces to make the necessary repairs. There's nothing like reuniting with an old friend. I've nicknamed her Rusty since she's not anymore."

I nodded and ran my hand along the non-clunker's spine, smoothing the newly sewn leather seat cover. "I sewed that for thee," Mom added with a wink.

"Rusty's amazing. Thank you, guys—I'm in love again," I said, honking the bike horn that was even louder than the Crusher's.

"Bugsy was there, nipping at my heels the whole time," Dad added with a smirk.

"Did you get hurt?"

"I'm glad one of my legs was in a cast. And you know what? I thought she had a mean streak, until I saw her new pups. A whole brood of little crazy nippers, tucked inside an old tractor tire."

Bugsy was a she? Well, that explained why she was so protective of her junkyard bungalow. With my rebuilt clunker, I'd soon be giving her pups a run for their money too. The daily race after school would be on with the next generation of Bugsies . . . could not wait.

Mom stroked Dad's arm. "All that time you were in the garage tinkering with tools, you were being sneaky, sneaky."

He nodded, grinning. "And there was something else—a double gift. When Bub said he heard scuffling, I thought he'd seen me in the front last night. I tried to be quiet, but it's tricky working in the dark with just a flashlight."

Huh? So, there were two secret projects in the works overnight. While I was climbing a hill at midnight to meet S1, Dad had been a busy bee in the front yard. Who would have guessed?

Chad and I exchanged glances, then fast-tracked through the snow, spotting Dad's footprints as he'd labored into the wee hours on his other gift. Rounding the corner of the house, we looked left and right, and then up . . . at the rebuilt ladder nailed to the trunk of our oak tree and the spectacular new *treehouse* awaiting us!

"Dad! A treehouse!" Chad and I yelled, in a mad dash to be first to scramble up the ladder. Thinking fast, I sidestepped and let Chad pass me, so he reached the ladder first. He glanced over his shoulder, delighted. So was I.

Once we were perched in our ultracool fortress, we peered over the wooden rail at the scenery of the surrounding town. I even spotted the hill where I'd been sitting mere hours ago.

"How'd you put this together in a single night, Dad?" I asked, in awe of his craftsmanship.

"I built it in sections in the garage, then brought them up, one by one, and pieced them together in the tree," he explained. "Learned that technique of partial assembly in the Marines— thank heavens my leg held up."

Mom placed an arm on his shoulder. "Doctor Bailey says the cast will come off soon," she reminded with a smile. He nodded, content. "Now, who wants warm pastry? It's freezing out here, you polar bears," Mom said, rubbing her hands together and hurrying back indoors.

"Beat ya inside!" Chad cheered as he swept down the ladder and toward the house.

I sighed and saluted in the direction of the hill. And to the west, I observed Christmas parade floats assembling along Main

Street, right in front of the park. The master plan was still playing out. Energized, I climbed down from the tree.

Heading inside, I kicked off my boots, hearing cries of excitement from the family room. "Bro, get in here. You gotta see this!" Chad called out.

I flung my jacket at the coat rack and rushed into the room. My parents and Chad—holding mugs of cocoa, one for me on the table—were nibbling Danish rolls and crowded around the TV. "What's up?" I asked.

They allowed me into their circle to view the PRN news special showing a stunning satellite image of Earth. "Isn't it amazing?" Mom said.

Yes, Earth is amazing, but the female news anchor was referring to something happening on the surface: "Last night, Christmas Eve, another remarkable event occurred in many countries that celebrate the tradition of Santa Claus and Mrs. Claus. For decades the rare phenomenon of *RSS*—or Red Solar Streaks—has been a mystery. But now an advanced panoramic satellite lens has identified the RSS as giant, glowing images of the jolly fellow, composed of countless red dots from around the globe, somehow projected into the sky. Fortunately, RSS do not interfere with any aircraft navigation. Check out this amazing satellite image from America."

The screen filled with the image of an immense red *Santa*, blanketing most of the country. We gasped in unison.

The news anchor continued. "Scientists have no idea how this happens and may never, as it lasts only several minutes each year.

Theories include pranksters, geomagnetic storms, or even alien hijinks . . . so stay tuned. This is Jackie Starr, PRN, signing off. Happy Holidays!"

Chad's eyes—and probably my own—shone with wonder as we watched the images of Santa lighting up the planet. And suddenly it all made sense. . . .

You see, Santa Claus resides in both fantasy and reality. His magical spirit lives inside of kids who believe, but also inside of the golden-hearted who create wonder for believers. And the two sides work in harmony, with a cast of millions, feeding each other with positive energy.

Together they play the game and become one . . . **S1.** Long live the S-Game!

I felt lucky to be drafted as a player. Infused with Santa spirit for the first time in years, I looked down proudly at my pair of red stockings. RSS had turned me into a believer once more.

* * *

We enjoyed a lazy breakfast in front of the fire, Dad poring over his new book and Mom busy in the kitchen. I asked Dad to share a few Marine exploits sometime, and he happily agreed.

"Hey, Chad, dare to race our mean machines?" I high-fived Dad, thankful for Rusty's new lease on life. "How much time before dinner's ready?" I called out to Mom.

"Ham's done in two hours. Be back or be sorry. Bub, thanks for fat Kitty, how did you—"

I nodded. "Just enough time for an adventure."

Donning his new gloves, Chad snickered as he rushed outside. "Warning: beast on the prowl!"

As I grabbed my jacket, Dad chuckled, enjoying our sibling antics again.

Considering Rusty had many years on Chad's new model, we were pretty evenly matched, racing neck-and-neck along our street. His Blue Beast created a streak of cyan in its wake, while I was falling anew for my amber polished friend. "Follow me, bro, if you can keep up."

"Oh, I can keep up!" Chad shot back.

I led Chad on my favorite ride . . . through the back streets to Sean's neighborhood, waving at him, around and back again to the woods and ramp over the river. Eventually, we made our way to Main Street, where the floats were coming into view. Inflatable Santas and reindeer and snowmen were positioned along the street. And leading the pack was a decorated platform on wheels with a real live Santa standing proudly, waving and laughing.

"Santa—S4!" I yelled, as we screeched our bikes to a halt on the side of the road.

Ray Mabrey turned around, back in his prideful place as an S4, wearing his original costume and a joyous red-cheeked smile. "Bub! Were you behind this?"

"Whatever do you mean?" I asked, biting my tongue, as we pedaled to keep up.

"I had a call last night at RSS, from a Mr. Dixon asking me to be Santa on the Clarke's float today. A dream come true." Ray jingled his bells. "Very Merry Christmas . . . ho ho ho!"

Chad gazed at me with sparkling eyes, then back at Ray. Undoubtedly, Santa magic was real—all it took was one look at my brother's animated face. "Is he a friend?" Chad asked.

"More like a comrade—met him at RSS, a special place. It's our last stop, c'mon." I waved goodbye to Ray who simply bowed his head in thanks, before turning back to the stoked kids lining the street. "But first let's swing by an awesome bakery to see an amigo."

Which we did . . . Chad and Joshua hit it off instantly, setting up a future sleepover at the Olney treehouse. Finally, carrying a fresh box of empanadas from Hungry Amigo Bakery, Chad and I cycled our bad boy bikes along the street to the RSS warehouse. "One more, please—the best!" Chad said, pointing to the box. "I'm starving."

"Later, dinner's soon . . . now one last stop," I replied before hitting the brakes outside of the warehouse. Skidding to a halt in front of the building, I could not believe my eyes! Slowly, RSS, Inc., was becoming shorter and shorter, actually *shrinking*! Lowering into the ground before our eyes. What was happening?

"What's going on?" Chad asked, gaping at my panicked face and then the giant warehouse being swallowed by the snow-covered ground.

I was helpless, completely at a loss. No rumbles or shaking, but it was like an earthquake was causing the entire building to disappear into a chasm. And that's when I saw her waving. Kip was standing on the rooftop of the RSS building . . . sinking, sinking deeper. Oh, no . . . slipping into the bottomless pit!

"Kip, hang on! I'll get you off!" Feeling a swirl of emotion, I ran as close as I dared.

"I'm okay, Bub. Really!" she shouted, oddly calm, with Hercules peeking from her backpack.

Alongside her were fellow Coreys, Jett and Austin, and Wahoo too. "What are you guys doing? You're falling into a sinkhole! I've seen movies about this. Jump!" I implored.

Chad just stood by my side, equally helpless.

But nobody leaped off. They continued their descent, standing with feet firmly planted. And with every inch they dropped, I could hear the dull, clicking sound of machinery. Was it one of RSS's mechanical tricks gone haywire?

"We're fine, Bub!" Wahoo called out, unwavering. "RSS is closing for the season. The operation moves underground till next Christmas—Mr. Mabrey's mechanical wizardry. But, never fear—once a Stockling, always a Stockling. There'll be more stories to tell."

Was she delirious? I gazed into Kip's lovely eyes and the faces of my friends as they lowered to my level. Even if they lived, I wouldn't see them for another year? I was crushed.

"Here!" I said, tossing the empanada box to Wahoo. "Thanks for everything."

She sniffed the box. "Hmm, smells great, even warm. That's payback—my sweet tooth."

"I can never repay you for all of your—"

"Yep, you can. Keep on being Santastic, Bub! Good sparks good . . ."

Wahoo hugged Kip and the guys like there was no tomorrow. Were they being brave to the end? I couldn't bear to lose them—in mere seconds, they'd be gone.

With a wink, Wahoo waved at me. A rooftop hatch opened, revealing Roy Mabrey, who grabbed the Stocking sign and ushered her inside. Did I hear one last "Wahoooo!" trailing off?

"I'll do my best, but don't leave!" I pleaded as Mr. Mabrey pulled the hatch shut. Still the building continued to sink, until it was barely above the surface. "Jump!" I yelled louder, hoping my friends wouldn't fall into the abyss.

As the warehouse finally dropped to street level, I observed the rooftop was emblazoned with a giant, red RSS logo, that morphed into a flat, vacant concrete lot.

With a loud metallic thud, the building stopped sinking, leaving Kip, Austin, and Jett standing right before me on terra firma. "You're not going too?" I asked, staring in disbelief.

"No, silly," Kip said with a smile. "We live here in town, just like you. I'm only ten miles away."

I could have hugged her, but just smiled goofily instead. Chad nudged me in the ribs and snickered. "But Wahoo—why is she going underground?"

"She supervises the operation; they work all year, building the toys. Santa hardly sleeps."

"But why would they stay cooped up for so long—in the dark? Like vampires."

"Because she and Mr. Mabrey and some Stocklings have a condition called photosensitivity."

"Huh?"

"High sensitivity to sunlight, that can cause really bad sunburn," Kip explained. "Haven't you noticed how they stay in the warehouse, only going out rarely in the day, but mostly at night? All of Wahoo's pictures were taken at dawn or dusk. Winter's the best time for them, as the days are shorter and darker. Rest of the year, they hole up in the warehouse in underground hibernation, then pop back up during the holiday season. Sorry, Bub, I thought you knew."

"And you're not allergic to the sun?" I probed, fearing the worst.

"Nope. In fact, I love soaking up rays." Kip beamed—naturally—a sunshine smile.

Austin and Jett edged closer. "None of the Coreys are photosensitive," Jett pointed out.

"It's why you were placed with us. We're the seasonal staff of the RSS team," Austin added.

"Does that mean you'll be back next year?" I asked.

"You bet!" Austin said, answering for the three of them. "And the next and the next and the next. Choc-nog breaks keep us returning . . . and a few friends."

Before they all could leave, I inquired if anyone wanted to go watch the parade. Staring down at my shuffling feet, I was hoping Kip would respond.

Checking his watch, Chad tugged my sleeve. "Bub—the ham!"

"Is that your nickname, Bub the ham?" Jett joked as the guys waved goodbye.

"If I'm ham, then you're spam. Adios!" I jested, glancing at Kip. "Uh, can't believe you live so close. I can bike ten miles in a flash. Maybe—"

"I'm planning on it," she said, blushing like me. "By the way, nice wheels, boys."

"Thanks!" Chad and I spoke in unison, accidentally bumping heads like two buffoons.

Kip giggled as she stepped forward. "Merry Christmas, Bub." She kissed me on the cheek and hurried off as I stood entranced until—

"Eat my dust, roadkill!" Chad began pedaling home, almost out of sight when I mounted my metal marvel and shouted: "Winner gets first dibs on the pie, bro. You have zero chance!"

For this young man, the story of my life was *sweet*.

* * *

Main Street was unusually quiet that Christmas evening, only a few sightseers out and about after the glorious parade.

At the Pet Project store where Patch was obtained, the lady owner arrived to discover a sparkly envelope slid under her door. Opening it, she found two fifty-dollar bills and a note that she read aloud:

"Barbara: Patch is very happy. Here's payment for him and one more giveaway. Believe! Signed, *Mr. S. Claus*."

The owner laughed and danced with joy as her operatic pets joined in the ruckus.

EPILOGUE

Twenty years later: The treehouse that Dad built was still standing strong in that mighty oak when the Olney clan returned for traditional Christmas dinner. Looking up, I nudged Destin—my ten-year-old daughter—and asked: "Care to check out the Santa Shack? It's a good day."

She stopped peering through her new toy Spy-noculars and ascended the trunk's ladder like a monkey, curiosity winning out. I followed behind, not quite as fast as I used to.

When I reached the treehouse platform, Destin was scanning the area highlighted by the low, winter sun. Within seconds, I spotted the silhouette of the hill in the park next to Main Street. I smiled while recalling that incredible Christmas Eve years ago, and all holidays since, spent with family and friends. We'd even celebrated my med school graduation with a treehouse ceremony.

Rich memories . . . more to come.

Destin spotted the sign that I'd painted in large, red letters. She turned up her nose and smirked. "Dad—Santa Shack? Why the name?"

"Ask Uncle Chad; he's an, uh, expert," I said, watching my brother wander from the house in his coat and earmuffs.

Chad inhaled fresh air, taking in the scene. "Chilly out here. Kip sent me to say cocoa is brewing, and Grandma's ham is ready at noon. Grandpa says loosen your belts, ha."

"Uncle Chad," Destin said, leaning over the railing, "Why's this called the Santa Shack? Remember, you're a physicist . . . no tall tales, please."

Chad grinned at the question and started climbing the ladder to join us. When he made it to the top, he pulled up his pant legs to reveal two red stockings. And I did the same.

"What are you wearing?" Destin teased. "Stockings belong on fireplaces."

"We're part of an, um, underground society that creates holiday magic," Chad explained.

"Nah, you're not." She shook her head.

Chad glanced at me, eyebrows raised. "A serious case of SDS: Santa Doubter Syndrome."

"She won't believe me either," I admitted. "Even when I say the Santa Shack is our secret base for planning golden deeds. Imagine if I told her about—"

"Santa can't be real, huh, Uncle Chad?" The onslaught continued.

I grinned. "Beware, bro—she's a brainiac like you, top of the class. Get ready."

"Wow!" Chad countered. "He brings joy and wonder to kids all over, and you don't think he's real? Santa energizes our spirits."

"Nonsense, plus all my friends say he's fake. Parents play Santa

. . . I mean, no human can visit millions of homes in a day even with GPS. It defies spatiotemporal continuity, right?"

Chad shot me a look. "Were we afflicted with SDS so young? She needs your doctor skills."

"Dad never talks straight about this. Even though Santa's boorrring, I need to know."

"Boring?" Chad sucked in cold air. "Okay, Little Miss Skeptic, here's the real deal: This Santa matter is not what you think it is. Not even close. It's about playing the *S-Game*."

"The S-Game?" She was clueless.

Chad grinned, eyes twinkling, ready to reel her in. "We'll let our friend explain it all."

"Friend? What friend?"

"A fine lady with pink power, one of a kind. Her name's Wahoo—she lives at RSS."

Destin leaned in closer. "Wahoo? RSS? Can I google those?"

I pulled out two black stockings and handed them to her. "No, top secret stuff—not even spies are privy," I explained. "Patience. All will be revealed. And please try these on today."

She eyed the stockings. Was this all a game? "You mean, Santa's not just a big fat fib?"

Chad looked her square in the eyes. "Absence of proof is not proof of absence. Play the S-Game and decide for yourself. Maybe there's a *real Santa* with a giving spirit and a vast network of helpers. If not onsite, he works behind the scenes pulling strings to make the magic happen. Nobody can be certain, but this much I know: Believing is sooo much fun!"

"Bring on Wahoo!" she squealed, eyes like saucers, heading back with pep in her step.

Suddenly, I recalled an old mystery. "Bro . . . remember that Christmas with bicycle wars? The best one ever 'cause it wasn't easy. Did you eat the Santa cookies then? Nobody else did."

Chad crossed his arms over his heart. "I was a brat, but not me, I swear."

I scratched my head, glancing at the northern sky. "Then who did? Seriously . . ."

* * *

Northern Arctic: Two Inuits heard animals panting, bells jingling, and a man laughing, as an icy vehicle landed on the downward slope of a snow-packed hill. Both men had seen the vehicle descend airborne—arguing, one pointed to the ascending slope while the other pointed skyward.

As the sounds of trotting hooves and harnesses commingled, the vehicle moved forward. Up ahead, barely visible through the raging blizzard, stood a massive red structure adorned with ornaments and twinkling, multicolored lights.

A lady in white awaited in the doorway. The jolly man in red stepped up to embrace her, then sighed. "Well, hello, lovely—I'm sleeping for a month!" They laughed merrily and walked inside.

The End